PRAISE FOR LIMELIGHT AND OTHER STORIES

" An impressive collection from Lyndsey Croal... full of sweet and sad, cute and creepy stories, along with a surprising number of pieces that feel just prescient enough to worry about.

REBECCA E. TREASURE, AUTHOR
AND MANAGING EDITOR OF *APEX MAGAZINE*

" A beautiful and haunting collection. Croal's stories tackle the big questions of our techno-capitalist age with clarity and compassion.

T.L. HUCHU, AUTHOR OF
THE *EDINBURGH NIGHTS* SERIES

" Lyndsey Croal's LIMELIGHT peels away layers of dreams and insecurities and presents them to the world. Poetic, and devastatingly sad.

DAVID NIALL WILSON, AUTHOR OF *WHEN YOU LEAVE I DISAPPEAR*

" Croal's superb story-telling pulls you in with a force as powerful as the rings around Saturn. This is sci-fi with soul: thought-provoking, contemporary in its themes, yet accessible even to a sci-fi virgin like myself. Everyone should read it!

CATHERINE MCCARTHY, AUTHOR OF *THE HOUSE AT THE END OF LACELEAN STREET*

" A gorgeous illustration of the intersection of science fiction and horror. Croal's stories are varied in tone and content: body horror, apocalyptic, speculative, grief horror - the whole gamut. Running through each is the author's distinctive, haunting voice of inevitability coaxing the reader from one horror to the next. Loved it.

LAUREL HIGHTOWER, AUTHOR OF *CROSSROADS* AND *THE DAY OF THE DOOR*

LIMELIGHT takes the most recognisable human experiences and asks 'what if?'. Birth, life, and death, and how familiar states might be altered in SF-style futures: Croal's short stories are delicately written and emotionally wrenching.

ALIYA WHITELEY, AUTHOR OF *SKYWARD INN* AND *THREE EIGHT ONE*

A sharp and incisive collection. A myriad of worlds await...from near-future science fiction and fantastical worlds that show our own world slightly askew, to far-flung futures and the distant reaches of space. Croal guides readers effortlessly through these vistas, showing the darkness beneath the mundane, but also the light and hope in the places that seem darkest.

A.C. WISE, AUTHOR OF *WENDY, DARLING* AND *HOOKED*

LYNDSEY CROAL

LIMELIGHT

AND OTHER STORIES

SHORTWAVE
PUBLISHING

Cover art and interior design by Alan Lastufka.

First Edition published September 2024.

10 9 8 7 6 5 4 3 2 1

ISBN 978-1-959565-46-8 (Hardcover)
ISBN 978-1-959565-42-0 (Paperback)
ISBN 978-1-959565-43-7 (eBook)

For anyone who has ever asked "what if"?

CONTENTS

NEAR

PATCHWORK GIRLS

She's died more times than she can remember. Been put back together more times than she can count. A patchwork girl, made up of replaceable parts. Her ability to die but not die should make her stronger, feel like a superhero, but instead, she remains fragile and weak, her whole life built only to be crushed as easily as a flower in bloom.

Usually, she doesn't feel the pain of the act. But this time, something has gone wrong—this time she feels it. As the knife slips between her ribs, there's a searing pain, a tightness, and then a coldness that spreads across every inch of her body. She shouldn't be able to feel cold. Not like this. She falls back, struggling for breath, while her analysis screams *punctured lung! Organ failure!*

The man who stabbed her stands over her, watching, holding her gaze, a twitch of a smile on his face. Is the trembling of his bloodied hands real, or is he acting? She can no longer tell the difference.

As she takes her last struggling breaths, she hopes that

when they remake her, they will give her brand-new parts. She can still feel the patched-up ache in her hip from the car accident, the one that had her bent in unnatural directions, bones sticking out of her skin. But this is worse, and she never wants to experience it again—this urgent gasping for air, drowning in her own blood. Have they changed her programming to make it more realistic? Or maybe she's dying for real this time. Maybe this is the end. There is some relief in that thought.

A bright light passes above her, a camera continues to roll, and the last word she hears as her vision fades to black is, "Cut!"

"They're so realistic," a voice says from somewhere far away.

"That's because they are," another voice replies. "Real body parts, even if they are lab grown."

"No shit," the first voice says, sounding more impressed than horrified. He pauses before he speaks again. "What about. . ."

Cold fingers touch her shoulder, slip under the strap of her vest, creep across her collar bone. She opens her eyes.

The man who was looking down on her jumps back. "Oh fuck, you scared me."

She blinks, just once, then sits up to survey her surroundings. Light streams in from skylights above, but the room she's in isn't her trailer, it's a warehouse, filled wall to wall with storage shelves, and humming refrigerators, with labels too far away to read. She's lying on a cold metal plinth in the centre of the space, the light breeze of an air conditioning unit goose-pimpling her skin. Her vest has slipped down past her shoulder, so she pulls it back up.

"Where am I?" she asks the two men, her breath hoarse. She pats at her side, feeling a tenderness in her ribs. She wants to lift her top to inspect the damage, but she's already feeling exposed lying in this big lifeless room, with two strangers, wearing hardly any clothing. One of the man's eyes tracks up and down her form, and she pulls her knees to her chest. "Where am I?" she repeats.

The man smiles. "Don't panic, sweetheart. We were just about to take you back to your trailer." She doesn't like the look in his eyes. It's the kind of look the men often get before they kill her, a hunger that says they want her, or need her, or something in between. A look that tells her they see her as nothing but an object to be used and discarded. "You're just in storage now, after the. . ." He pauses, as if unsure of the correct word. He settles on, "reconstruction."

"How long was I in storage?"

He shrugs. "A week, give or take. The film's all wrapped up now. You'll be onto the next one soon. That final scene was," he kisses his fingers and releases them to the air.

"Why did I feel it?"

The two strangers look between one another, then one raises his eyebrows. "Feel what?"

"The pain."

The other man starts to laugh. "Yeah, sure. You almost had me there." He leans closer so she can smell the stale cigarettes on his breath, the sweat on his skin. "We know you don't feel pain. But if you want to test it out, see if you can feel something *else*, I can help with that."

She doesn't reply, only shakes her head and looks to the door.

"You're even more beautiful than last time," he whispers.

She frowns, and her hands go to her face, but the features of it feel different than she remembers. They've patched her again, with a new face this time, so she must have a new contract, a new role to fit into. A starlet ready to shine again, just for long enough to meet an untimely end. She knows she's beautiful, but she wishes she weren't— wishes she was made for something else.

She slides off the cold plinth, steps away from the men, and shivers. She still feels cold, even though her body should be regulating her temperature. But still, she doesn't want to question these men more. And it's not like they would have the answers she wants. She just wants out of this place, so she lets them lead her back to her trailer. Outside in one of the studio parking lots, she passes a billboard where she sees her old self—the one from the last death—standing next to the male lead, him a poster boy holding a gun. She stands at his side like a shrinking violet, her eyes devoid of anything but pain. Why can't anyone see the look in her eyes and understand what she has to go through each time? Why does no one intervene? Why don't they *see* her?

She was sold to the studio ten years ago. Her model is a state-of-the-art creation, a body configured for a particular type of film. The ones with action heroes, or supervillains. The ones that need a beautiful woman to die as motivation for the male lead to save the day and become a better version of himself. And to make it more realistic, here comes a patchwork girl to die for real, on camera, in as many ways as they can think of until her body fails completely or lives beyond its warranty. That's when they buy a new model to start the whole process again. So far, she has died by drowning, strangulation, a cliff jump, a gunshot in the stomach (that was a slow one), being hit by a car (that one left the ache in her hip), and the latest: stabbed in the ribs (the one she actually felt). Up until now, it's been pain free—in the physical sense at least. But the memory of dying stays with her. She still feels that frantic desperation every time her body starts to shut down, every time she feels the numbness coming over her. She thinks that, surely, they cannot know the realism with which she experiences her deaths. And if they did, surely, they wouldn't continue. But often, other darker thoughts fill her mind instead. Maybe they do know that she feels what she does, and they do it anyway.

Sometimes, she tries to leave the studio between jobs. She has dreams of escaping, of living in the real world away from all of the glitz, guts, and glamour. During breaks, she will find herself walking in the wrong direction, away from set, or wanting to do something drastic as an act of protest. Just before a bus passes, she wonders what would happen if she stepped out into the road. Would the damage be enough to render her obsolete? Or would they remake her, just to die again on camera? Would they video her remains before they swept her away?

Other times, she thinks about running—running until her legs no longer work. She'll become stranded out in some desert where she'll die of thirst or hunger. And once she's dead, coyotes or wolves will pick at her bones until there's nothing left to patch back together again. It's a comfort to think of such ends, even though she can't act on them. Too many of her parts are inorganic and are therefore out of her control. Her programming prevents her doing anything the studio hasn't approved. Every time she steps too far away, something in her mind tells her no. *Don't do that. Come back. This is who you are. You were made to be like this. To play this role. There's nothing for you out there.*

And so she remains here, year after year, death after death, a perfect starlet, dreaming of one day leaving the nest while her wings remain clipped.

Live theatre is the worst of all. At least on a film set, there are only a limited number of people watching. But in live theatre, the spectacle is enhanced. Patrons pay big money for the privilege of watching her die. She hears them chattering as they enter the theatre, all abuzz with excitement and adrenaline. How will it happen, they wonder. How will she meet her end this time? The producers switch it up every show for the shock value. Last time, she had her throat cut. This time, she's to be strangled. But until her performance, she'll be sitting dutifully in her dressing room, assistants tending to her hair and makeup, making sure everything is perfect so that she can shine when her moment comes. So that as she takes her final breath

8

beneath the spotlight, she at least looks beautiful while doing so.

When she steps on stage and her killer approaches, she hears the intake of breaths from the audience. Some part of them know it's wrong, but none will stand up to protest, or intervene, or say enough is enough, and they definitely won't leave the theatre before the act is done. She wishes that just once, someone would take a stand for her, but none ever do. Instead, they all bear witness, some with hands to mouths, as if showing their shock will assuage them of any guilt, any complicity. Some look away as her limbs twitch and her eyes fade, but she thinks they are the worst offenders. To look away, and say nothing, so that when they leave, they are not haunted by the image of her.

Later when she wakes, reborn again in a cold lonely room, she imagines the audience gasping as she slumps to the floor dead, but she never gets to see that final moment.

She wonders if there's rapturous applause, or if people sit silently in grief of her passing. Are there any tears? At curtain call, do they think of her, or only the feelings her death elicits? The elation, the thrill that makes them hunger for more, come back a second time, witness a different patchwork girl play her part. Will they remember her name? The fake one they've billed her as?

Deep down, she knows that hers will be just another faceless death in a long line of them. The actor who killed her will get all the accolades.

One evening, she's put into a car by the director and driven out into the desert. For a split second, she thinks they're going to let her go, that her contract has finally expired, and she'll be rid of the studio forever. But when they arrive at their destination, a crowd has already gathered, most of them men, along with a few glamourous women. They're all wearing elaborate masks like the ones worn to a masquerade. They tell her it's just another job—a *different* type of performance—and that she's to smile and be on her best behaviour.

They sit her on a chair at the center of the crowd, which has now gathered in a semi-circle, and tell her not to move. Someone places an object on her head. *An apple*, she thinks.

One by one, the partygoers step up, choose a gun, and take turns shooting at her—they're supposed to be aiming for the apple.

Unable to move, she sits perfectly still as bullets strike her body all over. One strikes her thigh, which causes blood to spurt and spray. Another grazes her cheek and takes a chunk of her ear. With every shot, the crowd hoots and hollers. "So close!" they exclaim. Champagne is served to every guest, and the drunker they get, the worse their aim becomes.

She doesn't know if they ever hit the apple. She passes out before they do. She wakes up, however many days later, perfectly patched up again, healed from everything but the memories.

One afternoon, the director comes to her and thanks her, says her little act secured them the funding they need for the next movie, one that will surely be a hit. They've already cast the lead, the poster boy, and she will be his starlet. He talks through the script, but she doesn't listen or say a thing. She just smiles and nods occasionally, and he is satisfied enough by that.

In the evening, a bowl of apples is brought to her trailer, each of them rose-red and perfect, a sparkly ribbon on top. A gift from the studio. She stares at them but can't bring herself to eat one, wondering if it's the director's idea of a cruel joke, or if he genuinely thought she would like it. Over the course of the week, she watches them bruise and brown until they're rotten to the core. It's then that she throws them away untouched. A new bowl appears the next day, pears this time, ripe and good as new.

In her final scene in the latest film, she's tied helplessly to a post while the hero watches from afar, unable to save her. He screams her name, but that's all he can do. The villain's lip curls menacingly as he raises the gun meant to kill her. He's been told by the director to aim away from her heart because "that shit's too expensive to replace," so he shoots her in the liver instead. While she bleeds out, she gets an idea. It's something she's not tried before. Something so slight, that maybe, just maybe, she'll be able to summon enough of her free will to make it happen. A small act of rebellion.

As the pain from the gunshot subsides, and the darkness of death envelops her, she decides then and there that if the opportunity arises, if she is given the chance to save herself with this wild idea, she will take it.

It is three deaths later when she finally gets the chance.

She's lined up again for a reshoot because the lead

didn't act distraught enough at her last passing, and the studio now wants him to attempt to save her so that he can arrive just a second too late and cradle her in his arms as she dies. They want the audience to feel his pain, not hers.

But she doesn't mind.

Not this time.

Because this time they don't notice soon enough when she moves a little to the right as the villain fires the gun. This tiniest of actions causes the bullet to pierce her chest just below her left clavicle, and burrow deep into her heart. It's a pain like no other, as if everything in her body is burning all at once. And then it's just a numbness, like she's no longer part of the scene.

The director cries out, but she can't make out the words. The hero arrives at her side and holds her tight against his chest. There is a look of panic on his face, confusion. His hands feel warm on her skin as he uses them to try and stop the bleeding. For the first time since she's become a starlet, the leading man is actually trying to save her life.

She smiles.

Before the cameras stop rolling and the curtains fall, before she dies for the final time, she revels in an act that was all her own. She's no longer just a patchwork girl surrounded by poster boys. She's the star of her own life, and finally, she is free.

HUSH, LITTLE SISTER

When my parents bought Leia's Shimmer, they said it was for me, not them. But the last thing an eight-year-old needs is the hologram of her dead twin sister popping up at random moments, haunting her every move. I should have been allowed to move on, even if my parents couldn't.

Now that they're gone too, I'm standing outside the door of our childhood home for the first time in years, staring at my distorted reflection in the rain glass. I know she's in there, waiting. I've not seen her Shimmer in almost a decade. Dad said I was being stubborn when I stopped coming home at holidays, while Mum cried over the phone. But I couldn't be there, not while Leia was still around.

I take a deep breath and put the key in the door.

The hallway is smaller than I remember. Wallpaper peels at the ceiling, and a damp smell infiltrates the air, clings to my throat. The floorboards creak, and I look down. Leia's initials are still carved in one of them, in sharp edges alongside mine.

I'm about to head upstairs when she suddenly flickers in front of me.

"Bell Bell!" Her voice pierces, strikes me still. Leia was the only one who ever called me that, and it feels like a betrayal coming out of this programme's mouth. "I've missed you, Bell Bell."

"That's not my name. It's Izzy now."

Her face becomes thoughtful, dimples forming beneath her constellation of freckles. I'd forgotten how realistic her Shimmer is.

"Izzy. Hmm. Izzy, like Incy Wincy Spider climbed up the waterspout." She hums the tune, and it feels like a spider is crawling up my throat. "Your turn!" she trills, after.

"I'm too old for nursery rhymes, I'm almost thirty."

"Don't be silly, thirty is *old,* and you're three minutes younger than me," she says. "What's for breakfast today? Are Mum and Dad joining?"

It's almost dark outside. Her time algorithms must have got mixed up over the years—my parents stopped being able to afford the updates a few years back. After I stopped lending them the money for it.

"Mum and Dad aren't here. They're gone. Dead. Do you know what that means?"

She stares at me, face shimmering, then she turns and runs away. Her laugh that follows wounds me in more ways than one.

———

I'm gathering up Mum's old gardening magazines when Leia appears again. She sits, cross-legged on the sofa, body half submerged into the old worn cushions. The toy

Labrador she used to take everywhere sits next to her, its fur grey where it was once yellow, one eye stitched back slightly above its socket. Still, Leia strokes it gently as if she can feel its fur. My parents made so much effort to make sure a hologram was happy, while they were content to let my life pass by—my graduation, my engagement party. I didn't even bother inviting them to the wedding. They'd rarely leave the house for anything.

Once, they tried to trick me to come home, phoned Cal and invited him to dinner. Cal said yes of course, he's too nice that way, but when it came to it, we cancelled.

I call Cal now to check in and he answers with a gentle smile. "Hey there. How are things going?"

"Okay," I lie.

"Is she there?"

I angle the camera towards Leia, though she's sitting so still now I wonder if she's glitched.

Cal's face moves between concern and curiosity. "Are you staying there tonight?"

"Yeah. Just want to get this wrapped up as soon as I can. The solicitor's coming on Wednesday."

"Sure you don't want me to come?"

I shake my head. I don't want him to meet her. I don't want this to be the first time he sees any part of my past. "It's better if I do this on my own."

"What will you do with her?"

I shrug. "Can't leave her here for the next owners, and I'm not taking her with me."

"You're going to wipe her?" There's judgement in his voice—he's always been weird about this stuff. His dad keeps his mum's Shimmer, and he doesn't seem bothered about it. Doesn't understand my aversion, either.

"I don't know yet," I say to placate him. "She's not real you know."

He frowns. "I know, but just think about it. Once she's gone, that's it."

"She should have been gone twenty years ago."

"In twenty years, we'll be twenty-eight!" Leia says from the sofa. "Do you think we'll still live together, Bell Bell?"

"Bell Bell?" Cal says, smiling.

"Don't," I say. "Don't call me that."

His eyebrows arch sharply upwards, the way they do when he's upset. "Sorry. Speak tomorrow, then?"

I rub my eyes. I shouldn't have snapped. None of this is his fault. "Yes, sorry. It's just. . . this is all a lot. Chat in the morning, though? Love you."

"Love you too, Izzy."

I end the call and I'm left alone with my Shimmer sister, counting now on her fingers, over and over, as if stuck in a loop. I stand up to leave her to it, but as I do, she lets out a sigh, head tilting sideways, and says, "Love you too, Izzy."

I don't reply. Her programme must just hear phrases and replicate them. But then, as I leave the room she speaks again. "Don't you love me, Bell Bell?"

———

I'm woken in the middle of the night by a breath in my ear. I turn, and Leia's there, curled up beside me, eyes wide, staring. She smiles as I scream and jump out of bed.

"What the fuck, Leia!"

"That's a bad word. I'm telling Mum."

"Mum's dead."

Leia gives me the longest stare before speaking again. "Mum's just sleeping."

"No, she's not, she's *dead*, and so is Dad. And if you hadn't been here, maybe they wouldn't be." It's the first time I've said it out loud—the blame, the resentment I have for my Shimmer sister. If she was just gone, maybe they'd have moved on, had another life, one where they were proper parents.

Leia starts to cry, tears distorting her face. It's too familiar. She was always the crier between us. Dad would say I must bottle everything up inside, but really, I just didn't let them see me cry. They had enough to be dealing with.

"You should never have left us," she says through tears, then she sinks into the bed, disappearing.

The next morning, the man from the funeral home stops by with Mum and Dad's ashes. I take the urns and put them on the hallway table, then the man passes me another box.

"What's this?"

"Their Shimmer files." His eyes glance over my shoulder, where Leia's probably standing somewhere, watching. His expression is more bored than scared—he's likely seen a thousand Shimmers in his line of work.

I put the box next to the ashes.

"Make sure you register before the end of the month for the discount," he says. I nod and smile, just to get him to leave.

When he's gone, Leia wanders up to the table, twisting a curl of her hair between her fingers. "What's that Bell Bell?"

"Mum and Dad," I say, though she won't understand what that means.

But her face goes impassive, still. "I tried to help them. But they wouldn't wake up."

A chill creeps down my back. "What did you say?"

"I. . ." She pauses, and her Shimmer flickers as if the signal was disrupted. "Shall we watch a movie, Bell Bell?" Cheery again, as if nothing happened.

———

Later, as I'm cleaning out the shed, an elderly woman appears at the door. "Hello, dear. Are you the other daughter?"

I stand up and brush dirt and cobwebs from my hands. "Can I help you?"

"I live next door," she says. "I'm so very sorry for your loss."

"Thank you," I say, because what else can I say to a stranger who probably knew my parents better than I did.

"They were always kind to me, helped me with things in the garden and such, especially after my husband died." She smiles. "I'm glad you're here for Leia. Such a sweet thing. I never could afford a Shimmer for Harry."

I tense up. "Anything I can help with?"

"Oh, it's just Leia's in my garden," she says. "She likes to watch the birds, sometimes, but she's been sitting on the bench all morning, barely moving. I think she might be sad."

"Shimmers can't be sad," I reply. Nor should she be able to move past the house boundary.

The woman frowns. "Well, I thought you might like to know."

"Can I come over and see?"

I follow her into her garden where, right enough, Leia is on the bench under the hedge adjacent to my parents' house, staring up into the empty sky. "Leia," I say gently. "What are you doing?"

"Watching for robins. Mum says robins visit when loved ones are near."

It was something Mum used to say, but I only remembered her saying it after Leia died. "Time to come home. I'm sure that. . ." I turn to the woman, and she offers her name as Maura.

"I'm sure Maura would rather you didn't sit here all morning."

Leia turns her head in a strange motion towards Maura. "Didn't you hear me call for help?"

Maura blinks at her. "Sorry, dear?"

"They were. . . and I was. . . I called out. . ." Leia's voice is disjointed, strange. Her face is different too, features falling apart, one eye slightly askew just like her puppy. "On the night they. . . when. . . sleeping. . . just sleeping. . . I screamed. . . no one came. . . no one came." She begins to rock back and forwards. "My fault, my fault, my fault, my fault."

"Leia!" I shout, heart racing. "Stop this and come home." She stops rocking straight away, then her eyes blink rapidly as her face pieces back together.

"Oh, hello Bell Bell. I saw four blackbirds today." She smiles and begins to sing, "Four and twenty blackbirds, baked in a pie. Isn't it a funny song Bell Bell, why would you bake blackbirds in a pie? So silly, isn't it? Bell Bell? Isn't it?"

Out of instinct, I reach forward to grab her and pull her home, but my hand goes straight through her. My palm tingles, a coldness stretching up my arm. I retract it quickly. Leia doesn't seem to notice, she just stands up and skips off straight through the hedge until I can see her blue form leaning down over Mum's flowerbed, smelling non-existing flowers.

I turn to Maura whose face is pale. "Sorry about this, it won't happen again."

Maura offers a weak smile. "I'm sorry that I wasn't here that night. When your parents died. I wish I had been. I might have seen something, but I was at my son's up north. Leia. . . you will take care of her, won't you?"

I chew the inside of my cheek. "Thanks for your help," I say, and hurry home.

"You're not listening Cal. She had a total meltdown."

Cal pauses on the other end of the line—as soon as he answered, I could tell he was going to go into fix mode, instead of just listening. "How long since she's had an update? You said yourself that your parents couldn't afford it, but we could now, we've got savings."

"I don't need your money for this."

"*Our* money. We're married now. Till death do us part, remember?"

"Or after, apparently." I imagine an elderly Cal sitting with Shimmer-me in a countryside cottage, him reading a book while my imprint sits watching him, speaking a programmed phrase. "It doesn't matter. I'm going to get techs in to wipe her, it's the only option."

"Shouldn't you wait until you've had some distance, time to process?

"I didn't call for a therapy session, Cal."

He goes silent as if I'm one of his patients and he's giving me time to reflect on my words. "I'm sorry, Izzy, I know this is hard."

"I can't speak right now." I hang up.

It's late when there's a knock on the door. At first, I think it's just the wind and rain, but then it comes again. Leia's eyes had been fixed on the fire for the past hour, but she looks up at me now. "There's someone at the door."

The doorbell rings now, and Leia jumps up on the sofa, the bottom of her legs disappearing into the cushions. "A bell for Bell Bell, a bell for Bell Bell," she says as if it's a tongue twister. "A bell—"

"Stop it!" I shout, and she does. She looks away from me to the fireplace again, gaze intent on the flames. Leaving her there, I head to the door. I find a shivering Cal on the other side.

He smiles, rubbing his hands together, and peers inside. "Going to invite me in?"

"I told you not to come."

"You sounded upset on the phone."

"Of course I did, my parents just died."

"*Izzy.*"

"Cal."

He looks behind him at the driveway—just my car sitting there in the dark. He must have got the bus, walked the rest of the way. He rubs his arms and breathes into his hands.

I step out from the doorway. "Just come in. There's a fire on, so you can warm up."

He kisses me on the cheek, his coat leaving a dripping trail on the floor, and heads towards the living room. He looks inside, then frowns. "Forgot to add wood to it?"

I follow him, confused, finding the fire has all but gone out, barely an ember. Leia is where I left her, staring at the fire.

"How did. . . did you put it out?"

Leia frowns and starts pulling at a loose thread on her jumper. "Put what out?"

"The fire. There was a fire."

She shakes her head. "No there wasn't, silly Bell Bell. Fire is bad."

"There was, just a minute ago." I look to Cal, and he shrugs.

"Maybe the wind blew it out when I came in." He steps forwards. "You must be Leia?"

Leia turns her head so fast, her face blurs for a second, and as her features rearrange, she tilts her head. "Who are you?"

"I'm Cal. Izzy's husband."

Leia blinks once. "*Husband?*" She turns to me. "You got married?"

"Yes."

"Why didn't I go to the wedding?"

"It was. . . a small event," I say, though I shouldn't have to justify it to her.

She pouts.

"Don't cry," I say. "It's not a big deal."

Her expression wavers. "Why are you hiding things? I'm your sister."

"No, you're not."

"Come on, Iz—" Cal begins, but I cut him off.

"This is exactly why you weren't invited."

Leia walks up to him. "It's not nice not to be invited, is it Cal?"

Cal opens then closes his mouth quickly when he sees my face.

"I'm going to bed," I say, and march upstairs.

I'm getting into my pyjamas when I hear Cal and Leia talking on the landing outside. I listen against the door to the muffled chatter. Then, Leia is singing a lullaby, "*Hush, Little Baby*," and Cal is humming along. Why did he have to come?

I open the door, and he turns with a half-smile.

"Leia has a lovely voice."

"Had," I say. "Are you coming to bed?"

Cal stands up. "Good night, Leia."

"Will you read me a story? I can't sleep without one."

"You don't sleep, Leia," I say.

"I do!" She screws her eyes up tight. "See, I'm asleep."

Cal laughs. "I could read—"

"No," I say. "Just leave us alone, Leia."

She glares at me, then closes her eyes again, puffs out her cheeks, pretending to hold her breath. She used to do that when she didn't get her way, but I'm not reacting to it. After a minute of us standing in silence, she opens her eyes, then runs towards me. Before I can stop her, she's run straight through me.

It's like I've been doused in freezing water. "What the

hell, Leia." I reach for her, but she's already dissolved into thin air.

Cal walks into the room, putting a hand on my shoulder as he passes. "Reading a story might have been easier, you know."

I follow him inside and slam the door. "*This* isn't helping."

"Maybe you should go easier on her, she seems. . . upset."

I stare at him. "I really hope you're joking."

He shrugs. "I don't know, she's different to other Shimmers I've seen."

"What do you mean?"

"Look, it doesn't matter, I didn't mean to come here to make it worse. I'm sorry." He pulls me towards him. His clothes are still wet, but I lean into him anyway. He kisses my forehead. "It'll be okay."

A noise from downstairs wakes me up. Cal must be up and about. I head to the landing and stop, frozen. There's a hole in the top step of the staircase. And a body at the bottom.

"Cal!" I run down.

He blinks up at me, eyes rolling back in his head. Blood trickles from his brow. I put my hands under his shoulders and lift him slightly. "Can you hear me?"

He comes to after a second, then groans. "Iz. . . what happened?"

"The step must have been broken or rotten." I look up at the stairs again and my breath catches. Leia is standing at the top, fists clenched by her side, eyes narrowed in on Cal.

"I told him to be careful," she says. "This house is bad for accidents."

An unease stirs in my gut. "Did *you* push him?"

"Izzy, a Shimmer can't—" Cal begins then stops, putting his hand to his head.

"Why did you say what happened to Mum and Dad was your fault?" I ask Leia.

Her eyes stream again, blue crocodile tears. "I was only trying to help." Then she runs out the top floor window.

I turn back to Cal. "We should get you to the hospital, you could have a concussion."

He shakes his head. "I'll be fine, I'll just lie down."

"What do you think she meant, that she tried to help? Did she tell you about the stairs?"

"I don't remember. Maybe."

I help him to the sofa and bring a cold cloth for his head, sit with him, thankful that it wasn't worse.

After Cal falls asleep, I go to look for Leia. I find her in the garden, sitting facing the back wall. She's humming to herself, hands held out in front of her. There's a web in the corner, a large spider in the centre.

She turns to look at me, her head twisting in an awkward angle. "Did you know that when spiders moult, they sometimes stay beside their old body until they're strong enough to leave it behind?" she asks. "So, when you find curled up spider bodies, they're usually not actually dead, just discarded versions of themselves."

I frown. "I didn't know that."

She pauses as if deep in thought. "That's what I'm like. Except, it's like if the spider left its skin behind and part of itself too. And then the spider died."

25

My mind whirrs. Shimmers aren't supposed to be self-aware. "Leia, do you understand who. . . what you are?"

"You said I'm not your sister. But I am. Or I think I am. Though you're so much older now, and I'm not, and Mum and Dad got older too, before they. . ."

"What happened on the night they died?"

She takes a moment before speaking again. "I tried to wake them. They were just sitting on their chairs by the fire, sleeping really soundly, and I tried to call for help, but no one came." She turns to me, eyes unnaturally wide. "There was so much smoke in the room, from the fire, and I tried to stop it. But I couldn't." Her voice wavers. "It's my fault. I asked them to put the fire on, even though we didn't need it. I liked to watch the flames, and pretend to be warm, like when we were little. Remember Bell Bell, we'd come in from long walks, and sit by the fire, and Mum would read fairy tales."

I remember. The way I'd curl into Leia, with hot chocolate, imagining adventures in other worlds. I think about the fireplace, how Leia had stared at it so intently. "Did you put the fire out yesterday?"

"I don't know. But I wanted to," she says. "I didn't want it to happen again."

"And Cal. Did you push him?"

She shakes her head. "I didn't mean to. I tried to grab him, to stop him from stepping on the top stair, but I made it worse, and he fell."

I feel sick, cold. Maybe all of it was a coincidence—a gust of wind from the door put out the fire, then Cal just got a fright from seeing her and fell.

"I miss them," Leia says. "I just want them to come home, but they won't, will they?"

"Sorry, no."

She looks at the web again, touches the edges of the fragile silk. "Not even their skins?"

I look at her for a long moment. Somehow, Leia knows she's a Shimmer, with the memories of a dead girl. Somehow, she knows that Mum and Dad are gone, but that they could come back as something like her. Whether she's my sister or not, she's not just a programme. And I know now I can't just wipe her.

"I'm going to check on Cal, you stay here, okay?"

She nods, and for once doesn't fight me on it. I head back inside.

Cal takes my hand as I sit next to him. "You okay?"

I look over at the empty armchairs where Mum and Dad spent their last moments. The police said carbon monoxide poisoning was a peaceful way to go, at least. I squeeze Cal's hand. "I've been thinking. I'm not ready to sell the house."

He nods slowly. "Okay."

"And I might release my parents' Shimmers, like they wanted. To keep Leia company."

"I think she'd like that."

"That would mean we wouldn't have any money from the sale. And the house would sit empty."

"We can still visit."

I laugh.

His eyes narrow. "Why's that funny?"

"The idea that I'd visit my dead family more than my alive one."

"You've always had a morbid sense of humour."

I take a deep breath. "Did you know spiders shed their skin?"

"I guess, though it's the kind of random fact you forget."

"Leia didn't forget it. She didn't forget me, after all this time."

"Of course she didn't. Sisters are made of strong stuff."

I lie down, curl up next to Cal, and for the first time since my parents died, I cry. He holds me close as I think of my family gone, of all the years I didn't visit, of my Shimmer sister feeling alone with my parents all this time, with only the walls and the spiders in the garden as company.

The techs come to install Mum and Dad's Shimmers a few days later. The house is tidied, the top step fixed, but the rooms left the same, apart from the fireplace which I've had blocked up.

When the techs notice Leia's glitching, they offer an upgrade, but I turn them down. Leia seems happy as she is.

I don't wait for Mum and Dad's Shimmers to appear. I'm not quite ready for that. I say goodbye to Leia, tell her to be good, and promise that I'll visit someday soon.

Locking the door, Cal and I leave the house. Distorted through the rain glass, I watch three Shimmer forms embrace, my family reunited, happily forever and after.

RETIREMENT PARTY

At seventy-seven, Hank Arthurs was Rivers Corp's oldest retiree, a feat for any employee, never mind a manual labourer. To mark his years of service, the company threw a retirement party. There was cake, fizz, and a card signed by his colleagues—human and automated alike. Awkward chatter and office gossip made the rounds in hushed voices and subdued laughter. "Heard he turned down the Retirement Plus option," Hank's coworker whispered as he passed, underestimating his still perfectly functional hearing. He ignored the comment and forced a smile as the bosses and execs welcomed him. They were all forced handshakes and empty smiles; a feeble attempt at the appreciation he deserved. Not that he expected anything more from them.

The exec was a young up-and-comer, who'd likely only read his name on a form an hour before. He cleared his throat. "Let us celebrate the valuable and productive working life of Hank Arthurs. Fifty years and how many orders packed? Thousands, no doubt."

Millions would be closer, but Hank didn't want to admit it, hardly even to himself, so he just nodded, gracious. As the exec's speech continued, veering into an update on the company's latest advances, Hank tuned out and thought only about how he'd soon be joining Ida in retirement.

"It's not perfect, but it's better than nothing," Ida had said when he'd first taken the job, a step down from his previous exec role. "That's all we can hope for with things as they are."

"The hours are long," he'd said. "We'll hardly see each other."

"We'll have weekends. And this way we'll have a chance at a comfortable retirement. Then we'll have plenty of time together. You'll probably get sick of me."

"I never would," he said.

Ida only managed to work long enough for the Standard Retirement Plan, and though he'd been offered a Plus Plan, he didn't want to retire on his own. He'd join Ida with the Standard one with a few extra perks that they both could use, earned from his years of service. Then they could make up for all the long hours, all the lost time.

"So Hank, any parting words?" the exec asked at the end of his speech.

"Enjoy the fizz," he said simply, and his gathered colleagues raised their glasses, clapped, then mingled. Even the automatons held glasses and plates, despite lacking a digestive system. No need for breaks made for better workers. Social occasions like this were the exception, creating the illusion that they were equals. The automatons were indeed getting more realistic, almost blending in with the human workers – except their expressions were always slightly off: permanent fixed smiles, and eyes that looked both alive and dead, depending on the angle. He wondered if they ever had moments of clarity while in Work-Mode, thoughts of their own.

Ida might be present in any one of them, not that he'd know. She'd not be able to communicate with him in Work-Mode. Though, at least during non-working hours, she'd have some time in her own brain space—the retirement he'd been waiting years to join her in.

He looked now to the corner behind the fancy cake. The chair, prepared with needles and wires, where he'd take his last "living" breath. Best to get it over with quickly. He'd had enough of the party anyway.

He walked to his retirement chair head held high. The room fell silent. Watching, waiting. An assigned automaton took care with every step of preparation, binding him in place, inserting wires. He'd been told his body was still healthy enough to be stripped for parts, for use in the newest hybrid automatons. It would earn him some longer Work-Mode-free retirement time. Meanwhile, his eyes, lungs, heart, and even fingers, would be installed into the latest models. Hands newly wired, to never stop working. To never stop packing those damned boxes. He clenched his hands now as the automaton inserted the IV. As the fluid drip-drip-drip began, cheerful conversation filled the room again. Someone popped a champagne bottle.

An ebb of euphoria seeped in, and his skin felt suddenly soft, like jelly. The automaton positioned itself in front of him, face-to-face. Up close, it looked almost familiar, with its wide brown eyes. Human eyes. They blinked rapidly, and the face changed, no longer dead stares and sharp expres-

31

sions. It was softer. A smile at the corner of its lips. One he recognised.

"Hank?" The automaton's voice was gentle.

He blinked to keep the face in focus, head already foggy. "Ida. . ."

The automaton that might be Ida glanced behind, then moved closer. He could feel her breath: stale, metallic, mechanical. "We don't have long," she whispered. "I can only control it for a few minutes." She placed her hands—not Ida's, someone else's narrow hardened fingers—around his, and positioned herself to hide him from view. Though no one was even watching anymore. They'd resumed laughter and chatter, champagne flutes clinking.

"What's going on?"

She didn't answer, but something was tugging at his arms, his scalp. A pressure pulsed around his head. The wires, removed. The upload interrupted, along with his dream of joining Ida. But the toxins in his body were still working their way into his bloodstream. He was dying. And there'd be no retirement, after everything. He tried to sit up, but the automaton pushed him down.

"Ida, stop," he croaked. "I want to be with you."

The automaton wore a sad smile, eyes with non-existent tears. "I know, Hank, I'm sorry, but I can't let you," she said. "I won't."

"Why?" he croaked.

"This kind of retirement, they lied to us. It's no existence at all. It's worse than death."

"I. . . I don't care. Please. . . Ida."

"We'll meet again, my love, in another life," she said. "This will all have to end eventually. Then we'll have forever."

"You'd get sick of me in forever."

"I never would."

She held his hand, then, massaged it gently as his vision faded. Somewhere in the room, music was playing. A song he recognised. One he and Ida had danced to once, at an office event. Three years into working life, laughing, invincible, in love. Now that he thought about it, it might even have been at a retirement party.

RENT-A-BABY™: CONTENT WITHOUT COMMITMENT

Welcome to **Rent-A-Baby**™ for all your image and influencer needs! Rent one of our state-of-the-art models for events, day trips, or for revenue generating content creation, to experience all the benefits of parenthood, without the mess or the need to be tied down. Simply show off your new model and watch your engagement levels grow—online and offline.

Models can be customised to match with your lifestyle and personal preferences, including facial expressions and features, voice settings, and movement. Subscription options are available for longer-term needs.

If you're still not convinced, then read on to hear what our current customers* have to say about their experiences:

"Our Rent-A-Baby brings a whole new level of wholesomeness into our home life, helping us connect with new and bigger audiences. We chose a model suited to our minimalist aesthetic, and homesteading style, and it's perfect in every way. Everyone

loves the newest addition to our family. Between it and our Rent-A-Pet, we have more amazing content than we know what to do with!"

"With our busy schedules and daily pressures, we just don't have the time or energy to invest in the real thing. But Rent-A-Baby is effortless and has opened doors for us in so many ways. We've since made thousands from ad revenue and sponsorships, making the subscription cost well worth it. The best part is that no one on our channels can tell the difference!"

"Rent-A-Baby gave us so many different options for engagement, allowing us to expand our influence and followers. Now we have thousands of budding parents reading our daily posts and advice blogs, and we have some amazing products and companies lining up to partner with us. Highly recommend to anyone looking to expand their personal brand!"

Our future affiliated products, Rent-A-Toddler and Rent-A-Child, will soon be available, and you can expect some even more exciting features. These models will be fully customisable, with special skill or talent mods for that all important clickbait-generating content. Want to raise a musical prodigy, budding comedian, or dancing diva? Then sign up now to our newsletter to secure your waitlist spot—

perfectly timed for when you're looking to upgrade your Rent-A-Baby, which you can buy today!

So, don't waste any more time and unlock your influencing potential with **Rent-A-Baby™: Cute Content, Without the Commitment.**

Testimonials are anonymous to protect the identity of our customers—privacy is hugely important to us!

BETTER SELF

The first advert arrives in Callie's retinal display as she sits down for lunch. The usual options pop up to skip it: "take part in this free survey" or "subscribe now to RetinAd Plus, for an ad-free lunch break." She ignores them. If the algorithm records regular skipping, her personalised ad cycle will only become more intense—she made that mistake last month.

This advert is another diet one, the kind she's been getting non-stop since gaining some weight over the past six months. Yesterday, the ad had been for a mindful eating app to "reprogramme unhealthy food thoughts," but today they've moved to the harder stuff.

"Weight loss can be a hard pill to swallow, so why not make it easier?" comes a sing-song voice, as silver embossed letters 'BS' circle the display. "Swallow: the new life-changing product from Better Self ™. A pill a day will literally *swallow* your excess self away and train your body to adopt better habits. Sign up today at your nearest clinic!" A map appears with a pre-added Better Self clinic marker, only six minutes from her office. She recognises the logo, too—she's walked past the building enough times on her way to work. In the window, they have a moving AR display of beautiful people that look almost artificially generated—something in the way their eyes seem to stare right into your soul. Callie assumed they were just a plastic surgery and mods company, but they must have branched out into the clean-eating industry, too.

As the ad ends, with a, "Come and see us, you won't regret it!" she eyes her watery soup, a meagre attempt at healthy eating, then pushes it away. She returns to her desk and clocks on, restarting the timer after the break. At least she'll get no ads while in work mode, and she's lost her appetite anyway.

She scrolls through the list of service requests—the customers not content with the standard bot response eventually get filtered through to humans like Callie. She should be grateful to have got a customer service job in this economy—she's only one of six in her workspace now, where the office would have previously bustled with dozens of them. Still, it's not exactly made it easier for her—by the time customers get to her, they're angry and she's the one they get to direct it to. She steels herself, opens her service script, and accepts a request. She types, <<Thank you for contacting Cranium Technology & Services, how can I help you today?>>

<<Are you an actual human?>> they respond.

<< Yes, hello, my name is Callie. I'm a customer service assistant for Cranium. Please could you provide a quick summary of your issue.>>

<<Ugh, I've already been through this. You want it again?>>

She types the command from her list of pre-written responses—if she strays from the script, she'll only get another mark against her name. <<In order to assess your needs appropriately, please provide your customer information and a summary of your issue today.>>

<< God, you're a useless fucking robot. I hate this. I hate you!>>

They sign off after that, and she looks at the next message in the queue: << I think my CensorChip is giving me hallucinations.>> As she goes to prepare her response, she reaches into her bag and take out the packet of biscuits that she keeps there, for emergencies, and digs in.

The next ad appears while she's taking a toilet break. RetinAd, it seems, is always watching, always waiting for its moment—she can't even take a piss in peace anymore without being sold something she neither wants nor needs. She tries narrowing her eyes just enough to block it out, but a shrill alarm rings immediately in her head. "Please open your eyes," the automated voice comes. "To add eye-closing as a skipping trigger, subscribe to RetinAd Plus."

A RetinAd implant is one of the mandatory "perks" for a lot of jobs nowadays, especially in companies like Cranium, but unfortunately, the "Plus" subscription is a bonus reserved for techs and execs. Callie is a long way off from that. As the alarm becomes too intense, she rolls her eyes open and lets the advert play.

"Embrace change to your inner and outer body and

mind," it trills to her. "Swallow—a revolutionary new method for unlocking your Better Self."

The Swallow ads start to play continuously during her free moments: while commuting, showering, getting coffee, preparing for bed, or even with her morning alarm.

"What are you waiting for?" the ads ask her at the most inopportune moments. "Time to Swallow your body worries away."

"Weigh less, and you'll feel weightless. Transformation guaranteed."

"Go with your gut and release a Better Self."

The last time this kind of intense ad cycle happened, was with a special brand of cat food. The advert included a catchy little jingle sung by a cartoon cat that she soon found herself singing or hearing in her dreams—she eventually gave in and bought some just to make the adverts stop. Her wardrobe is now filled with high-protein cat biscuits, untouched, as the cat, unfortunately, didn't come as part of the deal, and her flatmate is allergic. After that, she stopped watching cute pet videos on her phone for fear of ending up with everything from cat litter to a special fur-removing vacuum. She wished she could get rid of the Better Self ads with the same social media purging, but somehow her RetinAd knew she was still a prime customer —unless she loses weight, or changes her lifestyle, she'll be stuck with the annoying reminders in her head every single day. Soon all she'll be able to think about are the Better Self slogans.

She blinks awake one morning as what feels like the hundredth Swallow ad plays: "Sign up *now* for a limited-time free trial."

Sleepily, she takes in the floating letters for a few long seconds, convinced she'd seen the BS letters swirling in her dreams last night. The ad continues, "As a bonus for your custom, if you join our programme today, we will include a one-month RetinAd Plus subscription for temporary ad-free living!"

As the ad repeats itself, she finds herself wondering whether the ads would stop if she ripped her eyes from their sockets. Or took the Q-tips from beside her bed and rammed them too far into her ears, just for a moment of quiet. She shakes the thoughts from her head. God, she really needs a break from it all, even a short respite. Some sponsored ad-free time would be better than the more extreme version, at least, so she rubs her eyes and selects the one-click-order, skipping past the Ts & Cs.

Her RetinAd flickers off straight away, and she basks for a moment in the first ad-free silence she's had in months. Listens to the morning birdsong outside her window. Hears the distant thrum of traffic in the streets below. Notices the laughter from her flatmate in the living room—her partner is probably staying over. Callie tries to remember the last time she even had a date, never mind a relationship. Since starting at Cranium and getting the RetinAd installed, she's not had the uninterrupted time to do anything for herself lately that isn't eat, work, watch endless content, then sleep.

She's about to go join in the living room when the

Better Self drone delivery arrives at her bedroom window. It knocks against the glass a couple of times like a disoriented bird, before she lets it in. It hovers up to her face, scans her eyes, then deposits the pill box into her hand. The box has a sapphire-blue sheen with the Better Self logo embossed in silver, the words *'Swallow your worries away,'* in beautiful lettering beneath it. The drone beeps, and trills, "Dosage must be taken before 9 a.m. daily to qualify for this introductory offer." It then floats there silently, and Callie waits for it to leave. She checks her watch—8:45 a.m.—and swallows the lump in her throat. She opens the package, pops the day-one pill from the foil packaging, and takes it with a glass of water. The drone bleeps, then flies out of her bedroom, onto its next delivery.

She's unsure if the pills are making her feel better, or if it's just the ad-free living that's to thank for the peace and quiet she suddenly seems to have—weight or not, she feels lighter, more relaxed.

She finds herself walking for long uninterrupted periods after work, enjoying the city without the constant drone of voices in her head. She even manages a date or two, meets up with her flatmate for dinner and drinks, and goes along to a pottery painting workshop after work one day. Is this how folks who can afford the ad-free subscriptions live? Disconnected from the tech-world, never knowing what they're missing out on. Maybe this is why her flatmate is so carefree—a "plus" subscription is part of the bonus from her consultancy firm.

To keep the peace and quiet for as long as she can, Callie dutifully takes the pills every morning and every night.

———

When the month-long trial ends, along with the ad-free cycle, the abdominal pain starts. Days of discomfort, accompanied by the restarted Better Self adverts, follow. There's an endless unease in her stomach, nonstop as though something is moving and clawing at her insides. She stops taking the pills, but the pain doesn't go away.

She tries contacting Better Self customer service, spending hours cycling through automated questions—interrupted by ad breaks—about the product, her background, and the side effects, suggesting at first that she must have a food intolerance or be suffering from a period of stress. When she finally reaches a proper customer service rep, they inform her that she's lost the privilege of specialist customer support as she stopped taking the pills without guidance. She gives up, hoping it will eventually subside.

But the twisting continues, and even her skin starts to act up, rashes across her cheeks and arms, and she scratches away as new adverts play in her RetinAd—Swallow ones again, trying to tempt her back into the programme.

After struggling through work for days, unable to think, unable to eat, she makes an appointment with a health clinic. The only one she can afford is an ad-sponsored one —most likely affiliated with a body-mod company—but what else is she supposed to do? Fully private healthcare would cost her an organ or two, which mostly defeats the point.

"It's unlikely the pills are the primary cause," the clinician suggests after her assessment. "Occasional abdominal cramping is common for woman of your age, nothing to worry about."

She clutches her side, trying not to wince at the stabbing pain that just shot through her stomach. "What about the rashes?"

"Stress, perhaps, you did say you've been having trouble sleeping too?"

She nods.

He pauses, looking Callie up and down, before giving her a pitying smile. "You may want to also consider losing weight."

She bites down on her cheeks, tasting the metallic tinge of blood. "That's what the pills were supposed to be for."

"Perhaps we can try a different dosage." He leans into his drawer and pulls out a shiny Better Self packet.

"No, I don't think—"

"This is the latest Swallow pill, minimal reported side effects," he continues. "It's a smaller dosage, but you can take them three times a day in place of meals."

She blinks up at him. "In place of?"

"Ah!" he says. "Swallow is a meal *replacement*. You shouldn't have been taking it with food."

She shakes her head. "I'm still not sure—"

"I'll prescribe it for a few months." He waves her doubts away as if he's only prescribing a mild painkiller. "We can follow up on how you're doing after that, though please don't stop taking the pills without consulting with a medical professional. Withdrawal can cause additional side effects."

She nods slowly, trying to swallow away any doubts. "How much will it cost?"

"Don't worry," he says. "I'll pop you on a payment plan, so you can cover it in instalments. Or you can sign up to our ad-affiliate programme. Your first few months will be covered but your RetinAd will play ads more frequently based on your personal preferences."

"Instalments is fine," she replies quickly.

As she leaves the clinic, pill box in hand, she notices a silver-embossed sign above the reception desk: *"This clinic is a proud Better Self Affiliate."*

Back at her flat, she pops the new pill out of the box. It looks fancier than the solid ones she took before—it's a small translucent capsule with a pale blue swirling liquid within. She pauses for a moment to watch the movement, then swallows it quickly as another ad for low calorie cereal bars starts in her RetinAd—unfortunately the new pill didn't come with another ad-free trial. Though, as the advert comes to an end, she notices the pain in her abdomen is subsiding, the twisting in her gut almost gone, now just a gentle pressure beneath her ribs.

That night, her flatmate pops her head in while Callie is lying in bed and asks if she wants to join her and her partner for dinner. But Callie isn't hungry—she has no desire to eat, so instead she lies there, doing nothing in particular, listening to adverts on her RetinAd on a loop, until it's time to go to sleep.

She keeps taking the pills dutifully at the prescribed times. The Swallow keeps her hunger and abdominal pain at bay. Though, without regular mealtimes and breaks to mark each day, she stops noticing time passing. She barely registers going to work, though her boss tells her one afternoon that her productivity is improving.

Sometimes, back at home, she's sitting as she's started to do, just holding her stomach, staring at the ceiling as RetinAds play in the background, though she's able to tune them out better now. It's in the quieter moments that she can hear a new voice. Not from her implant—it is a voice that sits nestled beneath her sternum, between her ribs. A familiar voice, like hers, but warped, almost like an echo. *Be better,* it says. *Almost there. Just keep going.*

And she does. When the time comes, she pops another pill from the pack, and swallows. And so it goes. Morning, pill, afternoon, pill, evening, pill, sleep, over and over again.

She soon forgets where the pills begin and she ends. Her routine is dictated by the daily Swallow cycles, the reminders pinging intermittently in her RetinAd. New ads accompany the changes—products for cosmetic surgery, skincare, and makeup, to embrace her full journey to being Better. She stops getting diet or cooking-related ads, though. Swallow has taken away the need for meals. Swallow has taken away the need for most things.

And in the free times between her pill cycle, the voice beneath her sternum continues.

You're doing so well. Follow your gut. Feel weightless. Keep going, Callie.

She is drawn more and more to mirrors. She will stand and stare at her shrinking reflection for hours on end. Though it never really feels like it's her that's staring back, it's her other self—the new one, the Better one. She holds the spongy skin of her abdomen and feels a strange swirling sensation in her stomach, though it's not painful like before. Sometimes, her skin morphs and stretches while she watches, as though something is moving beneath it, pulling every part of her in, tighter and tighter. It's strange, but part of her likes the feeling. She enjoys the way her bones have become more pronounced with each movement and finds comfort in the empty feeling in her gut. It is a feeling that stretches to every part of her, too, from head to toe. In a way, it makes it easier to just exist in the moment, removed from the growing weight of the world. Maybe it really could be this easy, to embrace the new Callie, her Better self.

Almost there. Almost. Be Better.

Weeks later, she's looking at her withered reflection when she notices a bulge in her abdomen. There's an unease building too, snaking upwards from her ribcage, expanding her sternum until she feels like her bones could simply break apart. She tries to swallow the feeling down, but it's not enough to stop the force now stretching up from her throat.

Almost there, the voice comes. And then she's saying the words from her own mouth. "I'm here. I'm ready to be better."

She gives into the feeling. Retches and gags. Chokes and cries. The tugging and pulling at her insides continues, and she wonders if it will ever end. She sinks to the floor, body writhing in the pain of it, wanting to scream, but unable to make any sound at all.

She doesn't know how long the stretching goes on for, just that at some point it stops. And finally there's no more pain. No more anything. Instead, she lies flattened on the floor, only skin and air, an empty husk of herself.

Then, above her, a movement. A figure stands there, inhabiting *her* body. No, not quite her body. She's like those AR ads at the Better Self clinic, the not-quite human versions of happy-looking perfect people. She is the Better Callie. The version of herself that the adverts promised.

Better Callie, smiles down, cheekbones sharp and high, shoulders square and unyielding. "It's okay," she whispers to floor-Callie. "You can rest now." Then, Better Callie walks out of the room, leaving behind what remains of her former self, melting away like liquid into the thin cracks between the floorboards.

PLEASE SELECT YOUR ISSUE

>>>Thank you for contacting the Artificial Companions User Helpline. Are you contacting us about a Companion you own? Y/N̶

>>>Please select your issue from one of the following options:

- Faulty Parts
- Mood Changes
- Altered Speech
- General Malfunction

>>>You have selected: "General malfunction." Please provide location details.

>>>You have entered: "Companion stabbed me. I'm hiding in shed outside. It's roaming the house. Please send help." Thank you for confirming your location. To proceed, please enter product details.

>>>Unfortunately, your details do not match our records. Where did you purchase your Companion?

>>>As your Companion is a second-hand model sold by one of our affiliates, please consult your affiliate user manual for support. Can I help you with anything else?

>>>You have requested: "Emergency Power Down." Power Down is only available to registered users. Please make a new request.

>>>I'm sorry, I don't understand: "My useless robot is trying to kill me. SEND HELP." Please try rephrasing request.

>>>You have entered: "HELP ME!!!" Unfortunately, no representatives are currently available, but we have forwarded your details to customer services who will respond within thirty days. Before you go, please rate my service from 1-10.

>>>I'm sorry I did not meet your expectations. For complaints, follow this link.

>>>Thank you for contacting customer complaints. Please provide further details.

>>>Unfortunately, I don't recognise: "Fuck, it found me. This is all your faulahfccccEEEE." Please try rephrasing request.

>>>Operation timeout imminent. Do you still require support? Y/N

>>>Operation timed out. Thank you for your custom. Have a pleasant day.

(UN)CENSORED

The dream must have been a bad one, even if I can't remember it. My hands are trembling, crescent-moon imprints in my palms, blood almost drawn. My heart thuds in beat with the click-clacking of the train as it rumbles along towards the next stop, uncaring of my nightmares. Up and down the carriage—people are staring at me. Either I cried out when I woke up or I spoke in my sleep again. Addie used to tell me that I'd wake her up by screaming, or crying for help, or even saying something sinister. I smile and make eye contact with a few of the commuters, and most look away and return to their business. No one wants to risk me starting a conversation with them, the strange woman on the train haunted by her nightmares.

I rub my head, feeling the tiny CensorChip embedded under the skin just above my ear. This isn't supposed to happen anymore. I tap my wristband—the holo-screen extends down my forearm—and scroll to check the Chip's status. All ticks and green lights. The description makes me want to rip the stupid thing out: *Connect to your CensorChip to free yourself from nightmares and hallucinations for a restful sleep. Cranium—improving the mind today for a better tomorrow.*

Addie warned me not to get a CensorChip, though she refuses to go to Cranium for anything, even a simple health assessment. I switch to my TherAppist to distract myself and practice my breathing exercises. Screwing my face up tight. Tensing muscles then releasing them. It doesn't work, and a woman across from me is still eyeing me cautiously.

I check the map. Still six stops to home, but there's a Cranium shop in two.

The Cranium shop gleams from the outside. Its moving window display advertises everything from purse-wrenching SkillMods to semi-affordable Focus ones. The Med ones—Cranium's latest market expansion since most hospitals were privatised—take up the left-hand side of the display, promising age-defying cell regeneration or life-saving Nanobot treatment. The number in front of the latter flashes red as it scans me: out of my price range.

"It's immoral," Addie had said when Cranium had announced their expansion plans. "If they're really all about this *'better tomorrow,'* then they should make it so everyone can afford it."

"But we *can* afford it," I'd replied, frustrated at her refusal to get help. "Don't you want to get better?"

"Why should I be able to access something that others can't? What makes my life more valuable?"

I'd not had an answer to that, but, unknown to Addie,

I'd already given into the marketing and had my Censor-Chip installed.

Inside, a shop assistant greets me with a beaming smile and cheerful tone, not a single hair out of place nor imperfection marking her glowing skin. "Hello Alexis, welcome to—"

"Lexi," I correct her, and her face freezes for a split second as she takes in the information.

"Hello Lexi," she says. "Welcome to Cranium, how can I help you today?"

"The latest CensorChip Mod I bought, I'm not getting the dreams or nightmares anymore—or at least I don't remember them—but I'm still feeling like shit afterwards."

"I don't understand the problem," the woman says, still smiling, eyebrows arched. "You want to remember your dreams again?"

I shake my head. "No. No. I just don't want the physical aftereffects. Can you fix that?"

The assistant pauses, her eyes wide and unnervingly still. AIs don't blink, but it's weird with the rest of her being so realistic. "I could offer you an in-app upgrade with built in METs?"

I blink at her. "METs?"

"Mood Enhancement Tweaks. They should help subdue the physical responses to your nightmares. As it's an in-app purchase, I can offer you a discount as part of our Flash Sale. Today only." She grins and her teeth twinkle in the fluorescent lighting.

I hesitate. I really do want to fix this. Maybe Mum and Dad would give me another loan. . . *no*, I can't ask them again. They're too busy with Addie. I'll pick up some extra shifts at the restaurant this week—I'll even be more productive if I'm not so sleep-deprived. Which means more tips. It'll pay for itself in the long-term. "Can you install it today as well?"

The assistant twitches her head in a single nod, almost like it's an accident. "Of course, just sit in our waiting room and a Tech will be with you shortly."

<Good morning, Lexi. Daily schedule initiated. Time: 9 a.m. Shift begins in two hours. Commuting time currently estimated at one hour.>

My eyes open as the voice reverberates in my head—the same voice as the woman in the shop, I realise for the first time. I rub my head. There must be a setting to change that.

I sit up and wait for the familiar vice to grip my stomach, the crushing weight on my chest, the shaking hands. But none of it comes. There's just a dullness in my mind. Has the upgrade worked?

I get up, make my bed, then sit at the dining table for thirty minutes staring into space until it's time to leave. I don't feel hungry, so my cereal lies untouched and soggy in the bowl.

At work, I move around the restaurant, one table to the next, not even stopping for lunch. I feel like it's going well. I've not spilled any drinks, forgotten any orders, nor argued with a customer.

Erin asks for a chat at the end of the day. She doesn't look annoyed, so hopefully she won't dock my pay this time. It's been a while since I've had a performance review. Maybe I'm up for a promotion.

"Hey Lexi. Some good work today. Looks like you got one of those Focus mods installed after all," she pauses, waits for my reaction, but continues when I say nothing. "Although maybe you could try a little harder with the customers, you know a smile here and there, a wee bit of enthusiasm about our menus. Just to show you're human."

I hesitate. "What do you mean?"

Erin places a hand on my arm. "It's just our clients expect a warmer welcome," she says. "If they only wanted efficiency, they'd go to one of the AI-run places, you know? We need to keep our authenticity, so they can come here and be free from," she waves her hand around. "All that emotionless tech and machinery. Do you understand?"

"Oh," I say. "I'm sorry, I didn't realise. I'll try harder tomorrow."

Erin beams, almost like the woman in the Cranium shop. "Wonderful, I'm happy to give you extra shifts, as long as you can keep that positive attitude all the time, okay?"

"Understood." I force a smile, though it feels weirdly wrong. Maybe I'm just having an off day.

Over the next few days, I find myself falling into a familiar routine: sleep, eat, work, repeat. But there are, at least, no nightmares. No constant exhaustion. No anxiety. Like the CensorChip is finally working, and this is my new normal. My *"better tomorrow."*

Another week passes and Erin pulls me up again after

my shift. "Look. . ." she begins. "I *really* tried to give you a chance, but this just isn't working. We've had some comments about your demeanour, and well, I think you should take some time off, find a way to rebalance or something. Maybe Cranium could have something that would help? You've got that CensorChip, right?" She points at my head, and I put a hand to it.

I'm about to protest, to ask for another chance, but then I realise I don't care. And I understand what she means. This week it's just felt like I'm going through the motions, like I'm watching the world pass by without being a part of it. "I'll try and get myself sorted out."

"I'm rooting for you!" Erin says. "I've transferred your last salary, though I've cut your share of tips from this week, given everything. I'm sure you can understand."

On my way home from the restaurant, I check my CensorChip settings. Everything says it's working properly —even the new METs are fully activated.

I stay at home on my own for the next few days, scrolling social media and watching whatever TV shows are on. If anyone were to ask me what happens in each episode, I'd probably not be able to tell them. But it passes the time.

The nothingness soon becomes suffocating. Like someone has flicked a switch in my head and taken away the very parts of me that make me a person. I've become robotic, monotonous. Just like the assistant in the shop.

I have to try to fix it.

The same shop assistant greets me with the same toothy smile and the same cloying voice that sounds like she's making a train announcement.

"What seems to be the problem today?"

"I don't feel anything."

The assistant smiles. "Is that not what you wanted?"

"No." I avert her gaze. "I don't want the negative physical effects, but. . . I still want to feel something."

"I'm afraid I don't understand. The METs deal with the physical effects of anxiety while filtering traumatic experiences." She tilts her head a little so that the smile becomes a bit less symmetrical. "If you wish to uninstall, I can arrange that," she continues. "However, it would come at an additional administration cost, and I'd be unable to issue a refund as you purchased this as part of our Flash Sale. It was all in the terms and conditions you signed."

I don't want to go back to the constant anxiety, the cold sweats, the feeling that it will only take one bad day for me to snap. "Can't you just adjust it?"

The woman shakes her head. "I'm afraid the METs we installed are the most updated versions in production. Any issues you might be experiencing are likely to be host-related rather than manufacturing defects. We can try installing another in-app modification," she pauses and taps away on the tablet in front of her. "Perhaps the SAD one might meet your requirements?"

I take a deep breath. "SAD?"

"Serotonin Activating Diffuser. The chemical to induce happiness. Never spend another day sad with this new creation from Cranium—enhancing the mind today for a better tomorrow," the assistant reads then straightens her back with a click.

"And if you install that, it'll fix this?"

She nods. "It will certainly help you to feel something."

"Fine. Install it."

"Delightful. How will you be paying today?"

I tap my wristband and open my account, ignoring the minus symbol in front of my bank balance. "Do you take credit?"

"Of course! Just fill out this form, sign here, here, and here, and you'll be all set for installation. A technician will be with you shortly. Thank you for your custom today."

As I leave the shop, my wristband buzzes. <*Mum*> flashes across my arm-screen. Smiling vaguely, I swipe it away. For the rest of the night, I walk from street to street until the sun rises and bathes the city in a beautiful orange hue. Energy pulses through me like an overcharged battery. I feel great.

I stop for breakfast at a café. A real human waiter greets me, brings me coffee with a smile. I smile back. What a lovely day. The wristband buzzes again. I answer.

"Lexi?" Mum is crying. Why is she crying? There's nothing to be sad about. "I've been trying to call you. Why haven't you been picking up?" There's a pause, and she sniffs, her voice breaking. "Are you there, Lexi? I can hear you breathing."

It's nice and warm in the café, and the way the sunbeams shine in through the windows makes the space look almost heaven-like.

Mum continues, her voice getting higher pitched. "It's Addie, she's. . . oh Lexi she's had a bad episode, we're at the hospital. The doctors have said. . . well, you just need to come to the hospital. We need to be together. Please—"

I hang up and sip my coffee. I think of Addie. Yes, my sister. We had a lovely childhood. Inseparable. How happy we were. How happy I feel now.

I turn my wristband on silent mode and walk out of the café without finishing my food, leaving double the tip necessary. All I want to do is explore this bustling beautiful city.

When a dog crosses my path, I bend down and wait for it to greet me, tongue lolled, tail wagging. Its fur is as soft as silk. I scratch it between the ears and speak to it in a squeaky voice. Its owner chuckles and says, "Lovely morning, isn't it?"

I look up at him, noticing a shaved patch behind his ear, a small lump just visible. "Yes," I nod enthusiastically. "It really is." Waving to the owner and the dog, I stride off in no particular direction.

The droning hum of busy traffic soon becomes soothing, as if the passing vehicles are like waves ebbing back and forth on a beach. Maybe I'll go to the seaside soon, walk into the water, and keep going, until all that surrounds me is empty blue. A car to my left makes a loud noise, and I stop. I'm in the middle of the road, traffic halted all around. The car is just inches away, and the man in the driver's seat waves his hand, shouts something, but the traffic noise drowns it out. I offer a friendly wave back. More noises come from the cars behind him, together in a beautiful symphony. I carry on across the road, thinking about how nice it is of them to stop to say hello.

When I reach my favourite park, I inhale the scent of ground coffee from a van nearby. I feel like singing, dancing, like lying in the sun and soaking up the warm summer air. My hand jumps suddenly to my wrist, as if I know I need to check my schedule, my messages. But it's a passing thought.

As it grows dark, I check the time. I've been walking all day. A dozen missed calls and several messages pop up. Frowning, I open the first.

<Lexi. Please answer. We need to talk. It's not looking good. I can't do this without you. Love you. Mum.>

I ignore it.

More messages flood in, but they don't make sense. It doesn't feel like it matters anyway. All that matters is that I keep living in this moment. If I stop, I might lose this wonderful feeling. I can't let that happen.

<Lexi. I can't believe I'm doing this over text, but what am I supposed to do if you won't answer? Addie died last night. I'm so sorry. The doctors couldn't do anything, not without insurance. We were with her. It was peaceful. Just call me or come home, or anything, please.>

<Lexi, you can't just block us out. This isn't okay. None of this is. I'm coming over.>

<I'm sorry I left that voice message earlier. I just didn't know what to do when you weren't home, this is all so hard. I'm not angry, I'm just sad. Are you sad? Your Dad and I are really worried about you. Where are you? I'll try coming over again tonight. Love you. Mum.>

<The landlord let us into your flat this morning and it doesn't look like you've been there for a while. Please call me. Even if just to tell me where you are. Please.>

<The funeral is on Thursday. I know this is very difficult, but you need to come home. You need to be with us. We need you with us.>

<I don't know how to help. Tell me how I can help. I feel lost without you.>

<You missed the funeral. Everyone was asking where you were, we're so worried. I've called the police. They've opened a missing person case. Please reach out. Please come home. Please, Lexi. We love you. Mum.>

As I read the last message, my wristband flashes red. I'm in the park again, sitting on my favourite bench by the pond. I feel like I've been here forever, watching as the sun rises and falls. I used to visit here with my parents and Addie when we were kids, feeding grain to the birds in the winter, watching ducklings grow in the spring, collecting fallen feathers from the edge of the water and pressing them into books.

It's a calming place. And it's mine now. Everything glitters with gold dust. Every sound flows in my mind with the most beautiful melody.

My wristband flashes and vibrates again. But I don't want it anymore. It's only a distraction. So, I take it off and throw it into the pond.

Everything feels just right. No hint of anxiety, no crushing sense of dread. Just pure, uncensored euphoria.

LIMELIGHT

Soft, calming music, played in the background as the AfterLiving clinician led Tom and his wife into the room. The office stood on a hill, elevated so it looked out over the city. The skyline was just starting to brighten with the sunset, and in the distance, the sea glowed with the reflections. It was a beautiful view, and yet Tom wished that he could be anywhere but here.

From the door to the right of the consulting room came a faint, steady beeping, and Tom tried not to think about what it meant. It felt like a clock ticking, a countdown, not long until there'd be no turning back.

"Now that we've signed all the paperwork. Let's talk about personalisation requirements?" the clinician said, her tone sounding too cheerful for the situation.

Beside him, Kay leaned forwards, hands clenched in her lap, hope ignited in her eyes. This was all his fault. After-Living had been a fleeting idea, spoken aloud on a whim while watching Nara one day, imagining what it would be like to see her wake up again. And now it was spiralling.

"What do you mean 'personalisation?'" Kay asked.

"Let's start with hobbies, skills?" the clinician said as though it were nothing.

"Oh. Well, she liked to sing," Kay said.

"Is she any good?"

"Yes. . ." Tom trailed off and looked to his wife. "Well, we think she is."

"She was average. She could hold a tune." His wife was already speaking of their daughter in the past tense, even while she lay breathing in the room next door. "It was a thing she enjoyed rather than an actual skill."

Tom shuffled uncomfortably, imagining Nara was here. What would she say if she heard them talking like this?

"We can make improvements. Add higher range, make her pitch perfect if you'd like?" the clinician suggested.

"No. Just keep her as she is," Tom said. "We don't need alterations, we just—"

"But Tom, she would have just *loved* to have sung better, wouldn't she?" Kay mused, her eyebrows arched sharply. Tom knew that expression well. It was the one she got when she was working on one of her design projects and just had a eureka moment. But Nara wasn't a project. She was—*is*—their daughter.

"Nara isn't one of your designs, Kay."

Kay bristled and sat upright. "That's not what I'm suggesting. It's a small change, what's the big deal?"

"Because, this wouldn't have been her path, would it, before all of this, so why would we—"

"It made her happy," Kay cut in. "Just think, now she

66

could be a star! A chance to achieve her dreams. Don't you want that for her, Tom?"

Tom flinched—was that really her dream? She'd always loved singing, but so do most young girls of a certain age. And Nara liked other things. He looked out to the view again, the sea now turning a deeper shade of red as the sun dipped low on the horizon. That's what she'd always really loved, being outside, by the water, the beach, exploring and going on adventures. Fearless. She should get the chance to be that again. "It's not about what we want."

"I want this for her, not for us."

Tom sighed. "But if we change too much, it won't be her anymore." Tom tried to take his wife's hand, but she pushed him away.

"No. None of this is her. She's in *there*, gone." Kay pointed to the door to their left. "But you were the one who suggested this, and I went along with it, so I think I should be allowed to make some tweaks to the final product?"

"*Product?* That's not, she's not. . ." Tom stopped, lost for words, and looked between the unmoving clinician and his wife. He glanced again to the door, where his daughter lay. He felt cold, tired. In too deep now, torn between wanting his daughter back and worried about what version After-Living would create. Maybe it would be okay to make a small tweak. She'd still have her own memories, thoughts, feelings. That's what mattered. That's what made her who she was. Wasn't it? He looked to the clinician again and gave a small nod. Kay beamed.

"Great, let's put singer in the specifications, then, add in a few vocal cord tweaks, increased lung capacity, and some tonal changes. But she'll mostly still sound like her, just slightly improved. Enhanced." Then on seeing Tom's expression, the clinician added, "Of course, it's plausible that a couple of years of practice and puberty could cause that anyway, so let's think of this as giving her a head start on getting back to normal."

"Normal," Tom mumbled under his breath.

"Thank you," Kay said to the clinician, ignoring Tom. "That all sounds great, she'll be so happy when she wakes up." Then she leaned over to look at the clinician's screen. "What about instruments? Maybe she could play the guitar, something like that? Round her talents out a little more."

The clinician nodded before Tom could interject. "I can install a programme at various levels of expertise. We could go with an intermediate level which would be suitable for her age, and she could develop her skills from there?"

"Great," Kay said. "I've always loved guitar."

"What kind of music does she like?"

"Folk or country," Tom said, remembering days spent dancing around her room. Blasting the radio on long car trips. Not minding when Nara sung the wrong lyrics because he always loved just hearing her voice, imperfect as it was.

"Though let's add something less. . . jerky. Pop, maybe, for good measure," Kay added, a gleam in her eyes. "Wider appeal."

The clinician made the adjustments on her tablet. "Great. Now, do you have any other alterations you'd like to make. Physical features, perhaps?"

Tom opened his mouth to speak, to say it wasn't necessary, but Kay threw him another stern look, and he quieted. As Kay spoke to the clinician, Tom sunk into his chair and stared at the door to his daughter's room. This wasn't right. But Kay insisted it was what Nara would have wanted.

Surely, if they'd had the chance to improve themselves, wouldn't they take the chance too?

Kay was in the swing of things now, listing new specifications and suggestions, so Tom instead focussed on the beeping from next door again, in an attempt to tune it all out.

". . .she was always worrying about that. . . how about metabolism. . . coordination, she was quite clumsy."

". . .a dance programme? . . .Yes, we can make those changes."

Once they were done, changing all the things their daughter had been self-conscious about, all the things that made her who she was, Kay squeezed Tom's hand and shook him out of his reverie.

"Let's turn this curse of the past few years into a blessing. She'll wake up a better version of herself, and she'll be happier for it," Kay said, and Tom found he couldn't argue. He gave his wife a vague smile and said nothing.

Nara's parents made sure she didn't remember dying as the machines were switched off, data nodes inserted, and the upload from AfterLiving begun. For all she knew, Nara woke up from a coma two years older, with only a slight memory of the accident that had left her sleeping through her formative teenage years. They'd even tweaked the memory data of the crash to be less traumatic, as the AfterLiving clinician had advised.

As the clinician brought them to the hospital bed, Tom saw something he'd once thought he never would. His seventeen-year-old daughter sat up and looked him in the eyes. Kay rushed over and took her hands, and Tom followed. He touched her arm, and her skin was warm. Her chest moved up and down with her breath. Her cheeks were rosy and there was no hint of the scar on her forehead. When her eyes focused and refocused, the blue was almost the correct colour. Almost. They narrowed and focussed in on them. "Mum. . . Dad. . . you. . ."

"Her voice," Kay said. "Oh Tom, it's her. It's really her."

"Where am I?" Nara croaked, then she turned and broke into a coughing fit. Tom looked to the clinician, who came and helped her sit up as Nara coughed up phlegm and specks of blood, but the clinician gave them a reassuring smile.

"It's normal, don't worry," she said. "I'll go and get her something for the queasiness."

The clinician left the room, but Kay didn't look perturbed, she was just staring at their daughter, eyes filling with tears. "Sweetheart, you came back to us."

Nara caught her breath and blinked, taking in the world around them. "Come back from where?"

"You've been ill, sweetheart, but you're all better now. All better, much better, in fact." She glanced to Tom. "Isn't she beautiful?"

Tom clenched his jaw. He didn't know what to say, what to think. This wasn't his Nara—he knew it in his gut. Even her mouth wasn't hers, altered from the slightly crooked one Tom had always found endearing—a fix request Kay had made. And when he looked into his daughter's eyes, he didn't see Nara looking back. He saw only a vessel and the dead eyes of his daughter's stare.

He stood up without saying a word and walked over to the window. He rearranged the flowers in the vase, sunflowers that used to be her favourite—maybe she wouldn't like those anymore either. He plucked a few petals off and clutched them in his hand. "It's. . . not her," he whispered under his breath as he let the petals fall to the floor.

"Tom," Kay's voice was sharp. "Come back here. Come and hug your daughter, for goodness' sake."

Tom ambled back but kept his distance from the bed as Kay touched Nara's cheek, moved her chin from side to side revealing the lesions and data nodes running down from her neck. Kay rearranged her hair—glossier than before—around her shoulders, then embraced her.

Nara peered around Kay's shoulder. "Dad?"

Tom avoided eye contact. Bit down on his cheeks, tasted blood.

"Beautiful. Perfect," Kay was saying. "Look Tom, even the scar on her cheek is gone."

Tom glanced at his daughter's face again as Nara touched her own cheek. She'd got the scar while climbing a tree when she was five—it was shaped like a dolphin, and Nara had always liked it, said it made her unique. She'd become obsessed with dolphins and the oceans after that, said the scar would keep her safe in the water. And now it was gone.

"She got that before the accident," Tom said, turning to Kay. "Why did you get that changed?"

"They really did a great job," Kay said, ignoring him.

"What's happening?" Nara asked, rubbing her cheek still, feeling for the indent.

"You're all better," Kay said. "All better."

"Mum, can you talk to me, properly. What the hell is going on?"

"Language please, Nara. I didn't raise a foul mouth."

Nara seemed stunned as she looked around the room. Tom noticed her gaze go to the mirror in the corner, eyes fixed on the reflection. Her face turned grey, and she leaned closer for a better look, touching every ridge of her cheeks, her chin, turning to get a better look of her neck beneath her hair.

The clinician re-entered the room, a cup of water and a pill packet in her hands. "Now Nara, how are we feeling about everything?"

Kay answered before Nara could. "We're feeling great. She's just perfect." She leaned forwards and cupped her daughter's cheeks again, smiling, tears in her eyes. "Just perfect."

"After-freak!"

The taunt came from the lunch hall table behind Nara, followed by half a soggy tomato, hitting her elbow before landing messily on her table. She tensed up, and turned, but Sammy put her hand on her arm. "Don't Nara. He's not worth it."

There was laughter from behind again, but Nara took her friend's advice and didn't turn. In the last few months since she'd come back to school after the coma, Alex had made it his personal mission to make her miserable. She'd expected he might be more understanding after the accident, but then she'd come back as a superstar student— better at everything, schoolwork, sports, and especially music. He hated her for it and didn't hesitate showing it.

"I hate him," she said hands clenched. "I just want to. . .
I don't know, do something about it."

"He does have a very punchable face."

Nara breathed out. "We were old family friends you
know, before the accident. Basically grew up together, him
and—" She stopped. She didn't want to think about Dylan
right now—Alex's older brother, the one who was driving
the car that made her like this.

"I'm glad the coma gave you better taste, then."

Nara nudged Sammy's shoulder, trying to tune out the
sound of more laughter from Alex and his friends. "Bit
harsh."

"I'm confident you can take it."

Nara smiled and let out a breath. She was glad that the
school counsellor had introduced her to Sammy when she'd
come back to school. Sammy was another AfterLiving client,
though it must have been harder for her. She was only five
when she almost drowned, brought back ten years later, all
grown up. Nara could hardly imagine what it must be like for
her—she struggled enough as it was with the two years she'd
skipped. But she liked that she wasn't alone in all of this. High
school was brutal enough for normal kids, never mind Afters.

"Why does he have to be such a dick now?" Nara asked.
"After everything."

"He just wants you to react," Sammy said.

"I want to react."

Sammy sighed. "The best thing you can do is show him
you don't care. Then you can get back at him by being
better than him at everything."

"I didn't used to be," she said. "Better than him."

There was another yell from behind, as a grape hit her

in the back of her head and burst all over her hair. She did all she could to resist turning as she brushed the fruit away, taking care not to uncover the data nodes as she did.

"Okay," Sammy said, throwing a glance behind her. "We need a subject change. What are you doing after school, other than feeling sorry for yourself."

"Rehearsals," Nara answered. She pushed at her own food on her lunch tray, appetite lost again.

Sammy made a face. "Skip them. Come to the cinema instead? There's a festival on. They're showing all the classic horror movies."

"That does sound more fun, but Mum would murder me if I didn't go."

"Who cares. You're your own person."

"I can't skip it."

"But you hate singing."

Nara frowned. "I don't."

"Then why do you look like you want to murder your entire family every time I ask you about it?"

Nara rubbed the back of her neck, feeling the scar on her hairline, and the smooth lines of the inserted data nodes moving up her scalp. "It makes my parents happy."

"Not your dad. He's never happy."

"That's not fair."

"Literally never seen him smile."

"Yeah, well at least my parents stuck around after—" She stopped herself. "Shit, Sammy, I'm sorry, that was. . ."

"Low blow, Nara." Sammy stood up with her lunch tray. "I know Alex is the worst, but you don't need to take it out on me." Before Nara could think up a response, Sammy marched away out of the lunch hall.

Nara's stomach sunk. Why had she said that to her?

Sammy's parents had left as soon as she turned sixteen, convinced she wasn't their daughter anymore, that she wasn't what they'd expected she'd grow up into. They still had the image of a sweet five-year-old in their mind, not the independent, cool, and edgy Sammy she'd become. *Fuck,* she'd really messed up now. She pushed her chair back sharply and stood to put her own untouched lunch tray away, but Alex was approaching her table, his bravado increased now that she was on her own.

"Lovers' quarrel?" he sneered.

"Fuck off Alex."

"Guess you Afters don't all get your happily evers."

"How long have you been practicing that line?" she said, and he grimaced a little. She tried to move past him, but he positioned his body in the way. Behind him, a few of his friends were watching, all whispers and sniggers.

"There's a rumour going around," he said, leaning in so close that the smell of his stale deodorant stuck in her throat. She stepped back until her thighs pressed against the cold lunch table. "A rumour that you've been altered."

Nara held her breath and looked for an escape route, or help, but the only people watching now seemed only to be enjoying the show. "I don't know what you mean."

Alex put a hand on the table behind her, blocking her in. "How else did you get so good at everything?"

"It's been two years, Alex. Get over it. Things change."

"Not when you've been in a coma," he said. "I think Little Miss Perfect might be Little Miss Altered."

"Let. Me. Pass." He didn't budge. She tried to move by him again, but he just pushed her back.

Alex lowered his voice, leaning in close so only Nara could hear his next words. "It should have been you, not him. He didn't get the luxury of being an After, so why should you?"

Nara tried to push past him again, but Alex shoved her harder. She fell back into her chair.

"Is that what this is?" Nara said. "Taking your guilt out on me?"

"*My* guilt? It's your fault. If it wasn't for you, my brother would still be here."

Nara struggled back to her feet. Her scalp itched, a pulsing inside her head. Then an image flashed in her mind. Blood and pain. Sitting in the car beside Dylan. He was coughing blood as he reached out to take her hand, said her name, then asked for his mum, his dad. Asked her to help him. And she remembered, pulling her hand from his, and then everything faded. A memory muddled—not like the one she thought she knew, the memory of them driving off together, listening to loud music and laughing in the car before the crash—he was taking her home from a party at their house, one where Alex had got drunk for the first time. Dylan had been tasked with driving her home when he'd come back with their parents. She hadn't remembered anything from the actual crash until now. Was it even a memory?

She clasped her hands to her head and looked up at Alex.

"What's wrong with you?" he asked. "You look demented."

"Just get out of my way."

"No."

"Please, Alex," she tried. But he still wouldn't move.

"I'm not letting you off that easy," he hissed. "Not until you wish you were the one who died in that crash."

"Dylan," she said quietly as the memory flashed into her mind again. "When he was dying, he didn't ask for you."

Alex's eyes widened. "What did you say?"

"Asked for me, asked for your parents, but not you."

"Stop it."

"Maybe it was because he didn't really like you," she said unsure why she was goading him, unsure if the memory was even real. But still, she continued. "Maybe he saw what others didn't. That you're just a pathetic bully."

"You bitch," he spat. Then, before she could stop him, he pushed her head forward, pulling at her hair, lifting her up. She struggled and screamed out as his hands reached for her neck, for the scar, and for the data nodes. Something kicked in as her hands balled into tight fists. She twisted around and punched him square in the jaw. It was a harder hit than expected. He fell backwards, and there was a sickening crack as he fell against the table behind, breaking his nose. There were a few screams, yells. Adrenaline rung in Nara's ears. Her hands were shaking, and there was blood on her right hand. Alex's blood. Or Dylan's. Her mind swum, and she was back in the car again, not the lunch hall.

"Just stop!" she yelled, wiping the blood on her clothes. "Make it stop." Her voice echoed in the hall, and she looked around. Alex lay unconscious on the floor, crumpled like a puppet with its strings suddenly cut. The rest of his group were backing away as if she might turn to them next. So, head still spinning, feeling as though she might be sick, she took her chance, left her tray behind, and ran out of the building.

"Nara, come in here right now and explain yourself!" Her mum's voice boomed from the living room as Nara walked in the front door. She stopped in her tracks. The school must have phoned about Alex. She was definitely in trouble. Probably suspended. What if Alex pressed charges? First Dylan, now she was going after the older brother. That's how it would be spun, even though Alex was the one who started everything. God, she hated him. Sammy was right— she shouldn't have risen to any of it. She shouldn't have provoked him.

Nara headed into the living room, putting her bag down on the chair. She walked up to her mum, letting her eyes drop to her feet. "I'm sorry."

Her mum let out a breath. "Just *sorry*? No explanation? You know how important these rehearsals are. The hard work I've put in to help you make these connections."

"Rehearsals?" Nara looked up, confused. "Did the school not call?"

Her mum shook her head. "We can talk about that later."

"But Alex, I bet he didn't tell you—"

"Your dad has had a word with the Morgan family, and they won't be pressing charges. They're happy to sort it out between us. We can deal with all that tomorrow."

Nara turned to her dad, but he wouldn't look up from his computer. It's what he'd been doing pretty much since Nara had woken up, barely acknowledging her existence. She was surprised he'd even taken the time to talk to the Morgans—though maybe that was all about protecting their image, not hers.

"I'm not apologising to him, if that's what they want," she said.

"Enough about that for now," her mum said. "These rehearsals are more important. This is your future we're talking about. You have so much potential, I just want to see you fulfil it, Nara, not waste it."

Nara paused. "I just forgot, okay." She was only half lying. After the incident with Alex, she'd run to the cinema where the film festival was happening. She waited there hoping she might see Sammy. But she didn't show. Then, Nara had headed down to the beach, to the rocks by the pier and stayed there till sundown. It was where she and Sammy usually went together—on warm days Nara would swim in the sea, and then they'd people-watch, listen to music, and drink beers Sammy had bought with her fake ID. She'd hoped Sammy might show up there, but she never did. By the time Nara remembered the rehearsal, she'd have already been late, so she stayed sitting in the dark and cold until the city lights flickered behind her.

"You *forgot*?" her mum repeated back to her.

"That's what I said."

Her mum's face became taut, cheeks sucked in as though she'd just eaten something sour. "What were you doing?" she asked. "Were you out with that Sammy again?"

"No. I was just. . . I was sitting, thinking."

"I can't believe you're being so petulant about this, running off, not taking this all seriously, after everything we did for you to make this happen."

"After everything you did for me?" Nara repeated her mum's words back. "What *did* you do for me?" She looked between her parents. "Did you and Dad have me altered?"

"Let's all take a moment," her dad interjected, finally deeming their conversation worthy of his attention.

Her mum blinked. "What are you talking about, Nara?"

"When you had my. . . when you had me made into an After—"

"Don't use that term," her dad said.

"Why not, that's what everyone calls me? An After. A freak," she said, her voice rising. "Alex accused me of being altered. But that's not true, is it?"

"Of course not," her dad said so quickly, as though he'd practiced the denial. He couldn't cover up the split-second look that passed between him and her mum, though.

"Then why am I better at things?" Nara said.

"You're just misremembering," her mum said. "The clinician said that might happen. Maybe we can take you to see her, have a look at your data nodes and memory files. See if something has got a little mixed up."

"Great. More tests, just what I need to feel more normal." She began to march away upstairs again, but her mum called back.

"We're not done, Nara. We still need to talk about earlier. About what happened."

"You do realise that you're angrier at me for missing a stupid rehearsal than for knocking Alex Morgan unconscious."

"Well, we can deal with it tomorrow, but it sounds like you had your reasons."

Nara let out a choked laugh. "Yeah, I did. But do you know what? I enjoyed it. I enjoyed punching the shit out of him—"

"Language, Nara," her dad said quietly, a feeble attempt at discipline, as though his heart wasn't really in it.

"I felt strong," she continued. "And I didn't know I could punch that hard, it just happened, and I liked it, and God Mum, why aren't you angry at me for it?"

"Maybe it's a side effect of the treatment," her mum said, lips pursed. "We'll go to AfterLiving first thing in the morning."

"Is that your solution to everything?"

"I don't know what else you want me to say."

"Fine."

"Fine."

As Nara left the room, her mum called after her, "Remember we have that audition for the reality show tomorrow night. And if you miss that, you're definitely grounded for the rest of the month. Which means no more beach, no more Sammy. No more anything you like to do."

Nara didn't reply. She marched straight up to her bedroom and slammed the door.

———

Nara jumped on her bed and screamed into the pillow, then she punched it over and over again, until her hand cramped up. It had only been six months since she'd woken from the coma, three since she'd been cleared for reintroduction. But her head still felt muddled. Every time she looked at her room, at any of her things from before, everything felt wrong, like they were from a life that was never hers. Even the photos of her looked strange—especially the one on her bookcase. She was stood between her parents on one of their trips round the coast, her dad looking like he'd never been happier, Nara with a slightly crooked smile, the dolphin scar on her cheek, and a slight gap in her teeth that no longer existed. She remembered that day like it was yesterday, and when she closed her eyes, she could even smell the sea, hear the chatter of seabirds above, feel the cool sand between her toes. She'd not seen her dad smile like that since she'd woken up, and her mum no longer looked at her in the same way. Sometimes Nara caught her staring at her with such an intensity, eyes narrowed, eyebrows sharp, mouth pouted, almost like how she was while in her studio working on one of her designs.

The visit to AfterLiving involved the standard tests and questions. Afterwards Nara sat in the waiting area while her mum had a meeting with the clinician. She sat thinking about the audition ahead and found herself scrolling through videos on her phone—clips of musicians, celebrities, influencers, all of them perfect in their own perfect lives. Or at least that was the part of themselves they showed. She rewatched a clip of a famous actress leaving a restaurant being hounded by screaming fans. She stopped to do autographs, all smiles and waves, but Nara didn't like the look in her eyes. She looked tired, unfocussed on the world.

Was that to be her future if the audition went well? It was what her mum seemed to want for her. But it wasn't what Nara wanted.

When she was little, she'd dreamed about being a marine biologist. She'd always loved being by the sea, felt at home in the water. Maybe if she messed up her audition, that could be her reality again. She could convince her parents to let her study for it, maybe even go to a university out of town, get a clean break where people wouldn't know about her past.

Nara's mum came out of the clinic cheerful and with the

promise there was nothing to worry about. Though for the rest of the day she didn't let Nara out of her sight, taking her shopping for the perfect outfit for later, going for lunch in a fancy health food deli. Nara tried speaking to her mum about the audition, telling her she was worried about it, that maybe she could miss it, but every time she did, it was like her mum pretended not to hear. Then before she knew it, it was time to go to the studio, and Nara followed her glumly inside.

The studio was a buzz of noise and lights as Nara was brought in. Techs and producers ran around, and she listened in while other candidates took their turns—teenagers like her: singing, dancing, showing off their talents. Did all of them want to be here? If they got selected, their life could change—thrown into a contest to become famous. Her mum had told her that this was her one shot.

Then it was finally her turn. A woman in a silver dress with a fancy earpiece and a tablet in her hands pulled her over and directed her to the stage. Someone handed her a guitar, and her mum mouthed for her to smile.

"Just do your best sweetheart, okay," she shouted to Nara. "I know you can do it. Be a star."

Then it began.

Nara had planned to mess up the audition—she would sing badly, or not at all. Make a fool of herself so they'd never ask her back again. But then when the time came, and she was standing onstage, bright lights shining, the eyes of everyone in the studio on her, it was like something took over her body. As if suddenly she was moving in the limelight without being a part of it. The lyrics and chords came out with ease, and she smiled, danced, laughed, and engaged with the audience or band at just the right moments. She did her best. Behind the scenes, her mum was beaming with her hands clasped together in front of her chest, occasionally whispering something to the woman next to her, the producer who made the decisions about who went through to the live shows. As soon as the lights blinked out, Nara felt dizzy. Her body ached, and when she took a step from the stage, her legs felt like jelly.

Her mum ran up to her. "You did it!" she said. "You're in the show. This is it. Your big break!"

Nara glanced over her shoulder. Her dad had arrived halfway through the set and was now sitting in a chair away from everyone. His eyes were fixed on a spot on the ground.

"You know, it was weird," Nara said, still feeling her body tingling uncomfortably. "I didn't even have to try."

"Shh," her mum hissed. "Nobody likes a show-off."

"No, Mum," she continued. "I wanted to mess up the audition, but when I tried I... I don't know, I just couldn't."

"Now why would you want to do a silly thing like that?"

"Because I don't want *this*." Nara waved her arms to the studio. "I just want to be normal. I want to—"

"Quiet, Nara!" Her mum pulled her sharply to the side. "Stop this nonsense. You have a gift, and it would be wrong not to use it. I know you know that deep down."

"But everyone hates me."

"They're just jealous."

"Everyone liked me before the accident."

"Well, let me tell you something." Her mum leaned in and whispered into her daughter's ear. "I like you better now. Before, you were average, and now you're great. Stop being such a diva and be grateful for the opportunities you have."

As her Mum squeezed her arm before returning to talk with the producer, Nara swallowed back tears.

Tom hadn't wanted the clinician to install the control option, but as soon as it was suggested, Kay hadn't even questioned it. Wasn't it every parent of a teenager's dream to have some element of control over their erratic behaviour?

"It'll help her," Kay had said. "She won't be used to her body, her life yet. That's what the clinician said. We can just give her a slight nudge, here and there when she needs it."

"We can amend the specifications as you need," the clinician had promised. "Just come back in and we can reduce or increase the intensity of the settings. It'll be up to you as her parents, for her protection of course."

Now as Tom watched the girl who had once been their daughter standing at the edge of the stage fighting away tears, his wife in her element as she spoke to some higher-ups in some industry he didn't care about, he wished he could go back in time. Wished he could have just let Nara go when they'd had the chance. At least then he would still have had the untainted memories of her.

Nara was booked on the show twice a week, which would increase if she made it far enough in the competition. School was not an option for the time being, so she was pulled out to be given private lessons on set between rehearsals and recordings. It was convenient given she had already been suspended, not that her mum even acknowledged it. The only silver lining was that she wouldn't have to see Alex anymore.

Every day she tried contacting Sammy, though. They'd not spoken since the fight at school, and Nara wanted to see her more than anything. She sent messages inviting her to the set, or asking if they could meet at the beach in the evening, but Sammy never responded. Eventually, tired of being ignored, Nara snuck out between recordings one day while her mum was away having lunch with the producer or some other publicity person and headed straight for the beach. She waited in their spot for hours until finally Sammy was there.

Nara cried when she saw her, ran towards her, and pulled her into a hug.

"Hey," Sammy said, gently taking hold of her shoulders. "What the hell happened to you?"

Nara took a deep breath and pushed her tears away. "I'm. . . I'm sorry about what I said, at school, but please, please don't hate me. Everyone hates me as it is, and I couldn't cope if you did too."

"I don't hate you, Nara, why would you think that?"

"Because you won't reply to my messages. You're ignoring me."

"I've not heard from you in weeks," Sammy said. "I tried calling round the house, but your mum said you were too busy. And I've been coming here most nights, hoping you might come to our spot, but you never did."

Nara felt ill, dizzy. "But I. . . I wrote to you, asked if you wanted to meet."

"Nara. No, you didn't."

Nara pulled out her phone to show Sammy, to prove it,

but there was nothing there. It didn't make sense. She remembered typing the words, taking her time to carefully craft what she wanted to say. But when she tried to remember actually sending any message, she couldn't.

"I swear I. . ."

Sammy took her hand. "Come on, let's sit."

When they were sat together, sheltered by the rocks, Nara digging her feet into the sand, Sammy put her hand on Nara's. "Are you okay?"

"I don't know." Nara felt the tears rise in her throat again. "There are things. . . I'm forgetting things. And sometimes it's like I just sort of zone out. I can't explain it."

Sammy looked her up and down then pushed her hair away from her face. "Is it your data nodes? Could they have been damaged somehow?"

Nara shook her head. "Mum's taken me to AfterLiving six times this past month, and they always say everything is fine."

"Just your mum?"

"Yeah."

"Your dad, what does he say?"

"He won't talk to me anymore. Won't even look at me," Nara said. "I think it was because of Alex at school, because I punched him. He hates me, thinks I'm an After-freak like everyone else."

Sammy cupped Nara's cheeks in her hands. "Look at me Nara," she said softly. "You're not a freak. You're you, and I think you're pretty amazing."

Nara bit down on her lip, then she leaned in and kissed Sammy. Her lips tasted of popcorn, salt and sweet, and for a moment the world stilled. It felt right, like it was a long time coming, and now it seemed like none of it mattered—

AfterLiving, the data nodes, her parents, the limelight and everything that came with it. It was just her and Sammy, and that's all she needed. She leaned back gently, and Sammy was smiling at her.

"I wasn't sure I'd ever get to do that again," Sammy said.

Nara frowned and pulled away. "Again? But this was. . . this was the first." Her first with Sammy, first kiss ever. Then there was a sharp flash in her mind, sitting with Dylan in the car. He stopped the car before her house, put his hand on her leg and leaned towards her, lips on hers. But she pushed him away—he was a friend, nothing more. Then he got angry. Started yelling at her, that she'd led him on, that she was a tease. He got so angry that he drove off too fast, wouldn't slow down, and then lights and. . . Her hands jerked to the back of her neck where her data nodes tingled.

"Nara, you don't remember?"

Nara shook herself out of it, remembering too much. That moment with Dylan wasn't how she'd remembered it before—the thought of it tugged at her gut, making her feel sick. It felt so real.

"Nara, are you okay?" Sammy said.

"I. . . my head, it's all muddled," Nara said. "Remind me. . . the kiss?"

Sammy brushed a strand of hair away from her cheek, tucked it behind her ear so that her fingers brushed the edges of one of the data nodes lightly. "It was a few months back, at the cinema. We walked out, stood under the archway on the promenade and it was such a clear night we sat on the beach after, watching the stars. And I saw a shooting star, you told me to make a wish, then when I looked back at you, we kissed."

Nara shook her head, looking down at her feet. It sounded so beautiful, so perfect—why couldn't she remember it?

"We went to see that ghost movie," Sammy continued. "And you said it would keep you up scared all night, so I said we could stay up together and it would be alright."

"I'm sorry Sammy, I just don't remember."

Sammy pulled out her phone and showed her a selfie, of the two of them wrapped in a blanket on the beach. She looked so happy, this version of Nara. How could she forget something like that? What else had she forgotten. "What's wrong with me, Sammy?"

Sammy took a deep breath, then she put her hand to Nara's neck again, brushed a thumb down the node. "I think something is messing with your data nodes."

"AfterLiving?" she said, then whispered the next part. "My mum."

Sammy nodded. "I'm sorry."

"Me too," she said. "I'm sorry I forgot."

"Maybe we should leave," Sammy said after a pause. "Get out of the city for a while. We can go anywhere you want."

"I can't."

"It doesn't have to be forever, we could come back when you're feeling better," she said. "We could just hit the road, travel for a bit. Get away from your mum. I've got money now from the accident settlement."

"You got that?"

"Yeah, when I turned eighteen."

Nara turned to her. "Sammy, I can't believe I forgot your birthday."

Sammy waved her hand like it was no big deal. "There are more pressing things than my impending aging."

"Like running away."

Sammy smiled. "Yeah. Like running away."

Nara thought on it for a moment. This could be a way to get her own life back, not the one her mum wanted for her. "Okay. Let's do it. But I need to do something first."

"Anything."

"I want to get my memories back first, I need to know who I am, what I've lost, from before, and from after."

Sammy looked at her for a moment, jaw working silently. "Okay, we should go to AfterLiving, they'll have it in your files."

Nara nodded. "When?"

"Now," Sammy said. "It'll be quieter at night, only like two people on security."

"How do you know that?" she asked.

"I broke in once," she said. "Back when my parents were trying to force me to be someone else, before they left. I thought I could go and fix myself, figure out why I wasn't like before. I thought maybe they'd had me altered, and it had gone wrong."

"Did they?" Nara asked. "Have you altered?"

Sammy took a deep breath. "No, they didn't. And I think that's what messed them up the most. They got their daughter back, just how she was always going to be, and she was still just one big disappointment."

Nara took her hand. "You're not."

"I know that now." Sammy squeezed her hand back. "And now I'm free of them, and really fucking rich." She smiled. "So what do you say, shall we go get your memories back then ride off into the sunset together?"

Nara stood up brushing the sand from her clothes before offering a hand to Sammy. "Lead the way."

The AfterLiving clinic looked different at night. Soft outdoor lighting lined the path to the entrance, and the glass building itself was dotted with only the occasional lighting so that it appeared almost peaceful. Nara expected Sammy to lead them to some side entrance, or secret way in, but they were currently walking straight to the front door.

"We can't just walk in, can we?" Nara asked.

"Of course we can, we're clients," Sammy said. "We just need to look like we're supposed to be here."

"What will we say?"

Sammy stopped on the path and let out a breath. "Okay, I've been thinking about it on the way up, and I have sort of a plan."

"You sound confident."

Sammy smiled. "It'll work," she said. "So, first you need to say you're malfunctioning, that you're feeling a tingling or something in your nodes. That will get you into seeing a clinician."

"I don't want to see another clinician."

"I know, but it won't be for long. While you're in there getting looked at, and they bring out your files, I'll cause a distraction and you can take the tablet with the data on it, and leave. Then I'll meet you outside and we can use it to figure out what's happened."

"We're going to steal from them?"

"It's not stealing, it's your data."

"If it's mine, then why can't I just go in and ask for it?"

"Because you're not eighteen yet," Sammy said. "Your parents would need to sign a release form, and do you really think they'd do that, given everything?"

Nara thought about it, then shook her head. "No. They wouldn't."

"So, it's a plan then?"

Nara hesitated. "Maybe we can just leave, without the memories," she said. "I can't ask you to risk this for me."

"You don't need to ask, I'm offering."

"We could get in a lot of trouble."

Sammy shrugged. "What are they going to do, put me back in a coma?"

"Don't," Nara said. "Don't joke like that."

"Look, it'll be fine, just follow my lead."

"I'm not good at lying."

"Pretend it's a performance," Sammy said. "Like you're on stage."

"I'm a singer, not an actor," Nara said.

"But it's still a performance," Sammy said. "Just maybe don't burst into song in the middle of the reception area."

"Noted."

"Or actually, if things are looking bad, maybe do. Spontaneous ballads must be a sure sign of malfunctioning."

Nara laughed, though part of her felt like she wanted to cry. "Sounds like a plan."

Sammy took her hand, and together they walked straight through the front doors. There was a beep as they entered, and the receptionist looked up from their tablet. "Can I help you?"

"We'd like to see Clinician Evans," Sammy said.

"She's with another patient," the receptionist said.

"We can wait," Sammy replied.

"What's this about?"

"My friend here, her data nodes are malfunctioning," she looked to Nara who gave a nod, then made a slight wince, before touching the back of her neck. Sammy gave her an approving look.

"They feel kind of tingly," she said. "Like static, or something." She wasn't entirely making it up—she sometimes got headaches that felt like that, usually after her performances, the ones she didn't want to do.

The receptionist looked sceptical, so Nara pushed her hair aside, and showed the nodes. "Just here," she said. "Something is wrong."

There was a sigh, then the receptionist gave a nod. "Your name?"

She took a deep breath. "Nara Miller."

"Nara Miller?" The receptionist repeated. He looked her up and down, then he eyed the corridor. Nara's heart was racing—this was it, they were about to be caught out. But then he only said, "My daughter loves you on that show. We voted for you."

Nara untensed her shoulders. "Thank you."

"She's quite talented," Sammy said.

"Didn't realise you were an After," he said, with an expression that looked almost disappointed. "Take a seat here now, I'll just make a call."

Nara held Sammy's hand tight as they walked across to the reception waiting area. She'd come to know every part of this space—even knew how many floor tiles there were. Thirty-seven to be exact.

"You're shaking," Sammy whispered as they sat in the corner.

Nara let out a breath. "It's this place, I don't like it. It all feels wrong."

"I know," Sammy said. "It's always so cold."

Nara nodded. "When I first woke up, everything felt so strange. It was like an out of body experience."

"I was the same," Sammy said. "One moment, there was the accident, next I was alive and well, in this weird room, ten years older with my parents staring down at me."

"Do you remember it, the accident?"

"Yeah, I remember it all," she said. "The boat crash, the waves coming in, pulling me under. It all feels so close if I shut my eyes and think about it enough." She closed her eyes and steadied her breathing. "It was dark, and I couldn't hold my breath any longer. Then I just remember opening my mouth, and my lungs burning for just a moment, and it was almost peaceful. Then. . . I woke up. It was so disorienting."

"I'm sorry it happened," Nara said.

"What about you?"

"It's weird," Nara said. "When I first woke up, everything was vague. All I could remember was heading off in the car with Dylan, turning the radio on, him asking me about school. We even made fun of Alex a little, that he couldn't hold his drink. I felt calm, like it was all normal, like any other day, and then it sort of faded to black," she said, piecing it all together. "But the last few weeks I've been seeing these flashes, of something else, of the accident. It's—well, it's worse than that."

"What did you see?" Sammy asked.

"There's this other jumbled memory. It was before the

accident. And he was. . . he stopped the car and tried to kiss me, but I pushed him away. It was never like that, or at least not for me," she said. "He got really angry with me. He drove off and wouldn't slow down. That's when we must have crashed."

"Nara, that's. . . God if he wasn't already dead."

"Sammy, he wasn't. . . he was still my friend."

"A friend doesn't act like that," she said. "He was a jerk, just like his brother."

Nara thought about the two memories of Dylan before the accident—both so muddled that she could hardly tell which one of them was the true version of him. A sharp pain hit the back of her head, and her hand jumped to her nodes. "Shit."

"What?"

"They actually hurt," she said. "The nodes."

Sammy raised an eyebrow. "Phantom pain maybe, like a placebo, being here. Guilt about telling a lie?"

Nara nodded. "Maybe that's all it is."

A door opened to their left, and clinician Evans was coming towards them. "Nara Miller?" she said.

Nara stood up. "Yes."

"Come with me."

Sammy stood up too, but the clinician held her hand out. "Just Nara," she said. "You can wait for her here."

Nara glanced back to Sammy, and she smiled to Nara. "It'll all work out," she said. "Trust me."

Nara smiled back and let go of Sammy's hand. Then she turned to follow the clinician.

Her heart hammered in her chest as she followed the clinician down the hallway. They walked past several doors, including the one to the clinic she'd first woken up in. Room six—she could remember that so well, but not her kiss with Sammy from a couple of months ago. There was another sharp pain in her head, like a vice tightening around her, a piercing pain in her eye. She closed them, and pushed her fingers against the sockets until the feeling went away. She wasn't supposed to be here, she should go home.

"All okay?" the clinician asked, stopping in the corridor.

"I. . . maybe I should go home, I'll be fine."

The clinician smiled. "You're here now, so we may as well try to get to the bottom of things."

Nara hesitated but nodded. "Okay, I suppose that's best."

She carried on, pushing past the pain and the sudden dizziness in her head, to the end of the corridor. As the clinician opened the door to her consulting room, Nara looked down the hallway—she half expected to see Sammy sneaking up behind them, but she was nowhere in sight.

The door opened, and Nara froze. There was someone else in the room.

"Hello, sweetheart," her mum said. "I'm very disappointed in you."

Clinician Evans shut the door, blocking the way, just as Nara turned to it. "You called my mum?"

The Clinician frowned. "She was already here, actually," she said.

"Why?"

Her mum pulled out her phone, and showed her a map on the screen, a GPS with a dot flashing bright. "I saw you were headed this way, and I decided to beat you here."

Nara froze, staring at the flashing dot, sitting right over the AfterLiving building. "You put a tracker in me?"

"It was for your own good," her mum said. "It's better I know where you are, so you can't get hurt again. All of this is for your own protection."

"You don't need to know where I am at all times," she said. "You can't."

"Who were you with?" Her mum's voice was like acid. "Because I know you didn't do this on your own."

Nara glanced to the door, wondering if Sammy had already begun her attempt at causing a distraction—maybe if she did, then Nara could slip out of here, run off. Then they really could run away together, find a way to remove the tracker later. "It's just me."

Her mum let out a sharp laugh. "It's that After girl, isn't it? Sammy?"

After. Is that what her mum saw her as too? Nara stared her down and said nothing.

"She's not good for you," her mum said. "How did you even get in touch with her? I thought she wasn't replying to your messages."

Had Nara told her that? "She's my best friend. I know where to go."

"Where?" her mum demanded.

"I'm not telling you that."

"You will. You *will* tell me."

"No, Mum—"

"Tell me. Now."

The back of her neck where the nodes ran up her skull pulsed again with a sudden burning. Nara put her hands to her head as somehow the words spilled out, as though her mum had reached into her brain and plucked them out herself. "At our spot by the beach. The rocks by the pier."

"And what were you doing there?"

"We were planning to run away together." Nara put her hand to her mouth. Why did Nara just tell her that? Her insides twisted while white lights danced in her vision.

"Thank you for telling me this, Nara," she said, then she turned to the clinician. "You see what we're dealing with here? She's only a child, we can't let her go running off with some strange girl we hardly know."

The clinician gave a tight smile and tapped away on her tablet. Nara felt another sharp pain.

Her mum leaned in close, and gripped Nara's wrist. "Now, you're going to follow me home, and not say a word until I say you can, understand?"

Nara tried to speak, to argue, but it was as though her lips had been sewn together. She started to cry, silent tears, as her legs jerked forward, following her mum from the room.

———

Tom was waiting patiently in the car. When he'd seen Nara walk up the path to the clinic with Sammy, he'd snuck out from the car park and listened behind a wall to their conversation, their plan. He'd considered warning them. Considered telling them to leave. But it wouldn't have mattered—Kay would find them anyway, now that she had the tracker installed. So, he just stood and watched the girls walk into the AfterLiving Clinic—let them go in, knowing their plan would fail.

He then sat back in the car with tears in his eyes as he

waited for it all to unfold. He pulled out a crumpled photo from his wallet—from before the accident. Nara was just six years old then, sitting on the beach, making sandcastles, decorating them with seashells she and Kay had collected together. Kay was off in the distance, waving, smiling. One normal, happy family. A few minutes after the photo was taken, Nara had jumped on the castle, and pretended to be a dragon, burying the shells within. Her treasure, she'd called them, before vowing to protect them forever and ever.

She had been his treasure. And now he'd failed to protect her.

Tom looked up again, just as the clinician led Nara up the corridor, where Kay would be waiting. Then, he got out of the car and headed into the reception, giving a nod to the receptionist who waved him in. Sammy was about to follow them, but Tom got in ahead of her and blocked her way from the waiting area.

She froze when she saw him. "Tom."

"Sammy," he said, measured.

"What are you. . ." then her eyes darted up the corridor. "Nara!"

"I think it's best you go before they come back out," he said.

Sammy shook her head. "No. I'm not leaving her."

"I heard you earlier. Planning to steal from this place, weren't you?" he said. "Then planning to kidnap our daughter."

Sammy's eyes widened. "That's not. . . you're the ones kidnapping her. She doesn't want to be with you."

"Go home Sammy, or I'll be forced to call the police," he said. "Or perhaps AfterLiving will decide to deactivate your data nodes, given your attempted crime here."

Sammy shook her head. "You wouldn't do that."

Tom pulled out his phone and began to dial.

"You're worse than her," Sammy said, voice desperate. "Worse than your evil wife. Because you're standing by and doing nothing while she does this to your daughter."

She was wrong—he was doing something. It was better for Sammy, not to get tied up in all of this. If he couldn't protect Nara, maybe he could protect her. "You've got ten seconds, then I'm making the call."

Sammy's eyes filled with tears, then she looked up the corridor. "I'll come back for you Nara," she whispered, then she left the clinic, and ran off into the night.

Tom sat in the waiting room until Kay and Nara came out. Nara was crying, but she walked forwards as if she was on autopilot. She looked up at him, a hope in her eyes, lip quivering, though she said nothing. In her eyes was a spark of an expression he remembered—a determination, a defiance. Then, in a blink it was gone. Tom reached out to her, but she flinched and walked around him. He watched as she scanned the room for Sammy. Her shoulders sunk as she realised her friend was gone. It was for the best. Kay would never have allowed Sammy to get in the way of her dreams.

"Nara, come on," he said. "Let's go home."

She shook her head, but didn't speak, though it looked like she wanted to.

"Nara." Kay's voice was sharp. "In the car, now, and stop those crocodile tears."

Nara's eyes widened, and the tears stopped almost immediately, though the expression on her face didn't change. Tom turned to the clinician and realised that Kay had gone further than he'd thought.

"This needs to stop, Kay," Tom told his wife when they were home. Kay had already ordered Nara straight to her room, and she'd obeyed her without argument. "What you just did... it's not right."

"I'm protecting our daughter. One of us has to."

"What's that supposed to mean?"

"You haven't done anything these past nine months. You won't even look at her."

"That's because. . . it's not her," he said, finally admitting what he'd been feeling all this time to his wife. "You changed her."

"I'm making her the best version she can be," Kay said. "When she's older, she'll see that."

"At what cost?"

"She's thriving, because of me."

"No, it's not because of you. It's because of her programming." Tom stepped towards his wife. "You've been going back to AfterLiving. How much have you changed? How many tweaks will you have to make before you're happy? How many memories do you have to mess with before she loses herself entirely?"

"Just enough to keep her safe."

"Safe or under your control?"

Kay shook her head. "I don't want her seeing that After anymore. She's all wrong," she said. "If her parents weren't happy with her, then she must be bad news. She'll lead Nara away from her proper path."

"Which is what? Fame and fortune doing something she hates?"

"She'll like it one day. I'll make her like it."

"Can't you hear yourself?"

"This is what I want for her."

"I'm leaving you," Tom said, almost surprised at the words coming out. "I don't want any of this anymore."

"Fine."

"Tell. . . tell Nara I'm sorry," he said. "Tell her I just can't do it anymore. I'll visit when I can, for her sake."

Nara tried to leave her bedroom as she heard her parents yelling downstairs. She tried holding the doorknob and twisting it. But her hands just slipped around the metal, unable to gain any traction. She took out her phone and typed out a message to Sammy, but every time she looked back at it, the words were gone, and the message hadn't been sent. Her phone rang, Sammy flashing up on the screen, but she couldn't seem to move her fingers to push down on the button to answer it. Couldn't even read or understand the texts as they came in—it was all a blur.

She tried to scream out in frustration but couldn't. It was as though the noises were trapped in her throat. Holding her neck, she ran to the bathroom and looked at her reflection. She traced the scars at her neck and scalp with her fingers. Felt the path of indents of the data nodes moving up her skull. The nodes that had ruined everything, had made her someone she didn't want to be. The ones that were now controlling her. She tried to shout out again, to test the theory. Her mum had told her not to speak, and now she was silenced. What else could her mum make her do? Her mind swum with the possibilities —her life was no longer her own. It hadn't been for a long time. But maybe it could be. Maybe there was another way.

Her hands reached to the medicine cabinet, and she took out one of her razors, broke off a piece of the metal. Hands shaking, silent tears falling, she held it to the back of her neck, pushed it down against the data nodes.

As the door slammed downstairs—her dad leaving—Nara made an incision. Then another. And another.

Nara woke to the sound of beeping. She was in the AfterLiving clinic again. It was almost like how she'd woken up the first time, except neither of her parents were there to greet her. She was distantly aware of the ache at the back of her neck, but when she tried to reach to touch it her arms didn't—*couldn't*—stretch that far. She stood up slowly and hobbled over to the other side of the room where a full-length mirror stood. The reflection that stared back at her felt all wrong. Her face was more angular, her eyes rounder, her cheeks thinner. Even her mouth was upturned slightly so she seemed almost to be permanently smiling. She barely recognised herself. The door opened and her mum stepped in.

"Oh thank goodness you're awake, sweetheart."

"Mum," she mumbled, feeling like there was grit in her throat. "What happened?"

"You slipped, had a fall, but you're all fixed up now."

"I. . . fell." Nara searched for the memory of it in her mind, but everything was blank.

"How are you feeling?" her mum took her hands, squeezed her palms lightly.

"Tired. Sore," she said. "What day is it? I feel like. . . I was supposed to do something. I'm supposed to be somewhere else." She thought about the day before, about plans she might have made, but every time her mind settled on something her thoughts slipped away. Her hand twitched to her pocket, but her phone was no longer there. She had an urge to message someone, to call them, but she couldn't remember who, nor why.

"Can I help?"

"I can't remember."

"That's okay, the clinician said things might be a bit foggy for a while."

Nara nodded, looking out the window to the sea in the distance. "Where's Dad?"

"He's on his way back, he'll be here soon."

"Back from where?"

"Oh, it doesn't matter. It's all in the past now."

"Can I speak to him?"

"Of course, but he's going to get some help from After-Living first, isn't that great?" she said. "He's been struggling with a few things lately, but don't worry, he'll be here again in time for your big show."

"Big show?"

"Yes, you have a special one this weekend, Nara. You're the opening act, your first solo performance," she said. "You are feeling better, now, aren't you?"

"I. . . I don't know. I don't—"

"Nara." Her mum's tone was harsh, her eyes narrowed. "You *are* feeling better."

Nara sucked in a breath. "I. . . yes, I am. Yes. I'm feeling better. Much better."

"And you will be able to sing."

"Yes, I'll be able to sing."

Her mum grinned and squeezed Nara's hands again. "Shall we talk about the set list? The studio sent over the requirements, but I thought maybe we might like to add some extras in. It's the personalisation that makes all the difference."

Nara blinked and thought about being in the limelight again, about her audition, and all the shows, and how she only wanted to go away, to be somewhere else, even if she couldn't remember where. "I don't want. . . I don't. . ." But she couldn't voice her concerns.

"Nara, sweetheart, there's really no need to worry," her mum said. "You're going to do great. They're going to love you. You're going to be a star."

"Yes," Nara said. "They're going to love me. I'm going to be a star."

F
A
R

WE MAINTAIN THE MOONS

Helix leaves his dome just before second-set, the time of the day when the Disk's tilt brings a slight shimmer of red to the distant horizon. It's the warmest part of the day, though frost still spiderwebs across his metallic limbs with every step. He's feeling stiff today—he'll have to do some maintenance exercises once he gets to his anchor.

Days and nights have always been this cold and dark in the Big Freeze. The Disk's star doesn't reach the far edges so instead the phantom moons light the way, reflecting amber across endless ice sheets. Most in the Hab Zones believe nothing can survive in the Big Freeze, but there is a town here. Metal and ice, stalwart in the night-frozen-sea.

Helix has resided here for over a decade now, since he was assigned his first real job after the Act was passed. At the time of the change, he'd hoped he might pick up something more glamourous—an architect, engineer, or maybe even an astronaut. But inner jobs were filled quickly by more up to date models than his own, relegating him to become a Big Freeze outlaw. Though, he is an outlaw with a purpose, at least. Such is the life of a Maintainer.

The inners might look down on the outers, but those in the Hab Zones really don't understand how much they need the recruits like Helix in the Big Freeze. Maintainers keep the myriad moon anchors safe, so that the Disk keeps spinning, tides still break, and gravity doesn't fail, sending them drifting into the unknown. If those in the inner circles knew, there'd be a panic, so this is a burden the Maintainers alone must hold.

We maintain the moons.

As he walks to his assigned anchor, Helix begins one of his Disk cartography studies, an activity he does most days to pass the time on his commute. First, he identifies a Hab Zone settlement at random, a place due west from here, then downloads the information about it from his data archives. There's even a radio channel which he can tune into, so he listens to the folk-rock music that's currently playing as he sorts through the rest of the data. The town is known for its ice fishing, just on the edges of the Big Freeze. It has a decent-sized population of a few thousand, and most workers are fishers and ice harvesters, though with a lower robot-to-human ratio than average. One of the more traditional places. He calculates how long it would take to walk there: just one-hundred and seven days, eight hours, and sixteen minutes, give or take (plus time for maintenance and recharge).

Sometimes he finds himself imagining if he could ever make the shift back to a Hab Zone settlement like that, to a different life once his current contract ends. Though after breaking from the years of service in the inners, being a Maintainer has been the only job he's been able to find that actually gives him this kind of meaning. That's how the Maintainers recruited him in the first place. Offered him the promise of a stable life, a home and generous salary, and a real purpose to serve the Disk. The catch: a life spent in the cold and dark. Though after a decade or so, he's found he quite likes the quiet structured life, and the dark doesn't bother him as much as it seems to bother the human Maintainers. He gets his charging needs fulfilled during his moon runs, and he likes the community they've built here in the vast frozen dregs of the world. People accept and value him here—a town of Maintainers, with robots, humans, and their families alike, living in relative harmony. It was a different story in the inner cities, where you could walk up and down the street and never be noticed or acknowledged once, blending into the background blur of a fast-moving city. In its way, it was even more lonely than this vast frozen ice plain.

—————

Helix arrives at his assigned anchor as the red sky fades into black. He stretches, as above him his phantom moon begins to glow bright. It's a crescent setting today. Phases give the illusion of a cyclical life. One of the bulbs is out, though—not something your average inner would notice, but his eyes have been trained over time to spot the smallest of gaps. His town leader says he's got the best eye of even the outers, something he takes lots of pride in.

The anchor creaks as he steps into the maintenance pod and attaches his own cable anchor to the wall. The lift ascends into the dark with a familiar tug as the pod speeds up and gravity drops away. He lets himself float weightless for a while, starfishes his limbs until the pod stops at the main moon-port. Still anchored to the pod, he floats into the space beyond, then up into the structure of the phantom moon. He finds his way to the broken bulb and replaces it carefully. After, he checks the solar panels, fusion engines, and the upper anchor holds. All is as it should be.

When he's done, he floats cross-legged, suspended over the edge of the port. The moon bulbs brighten the space around him, and he watches the Disk below. He enjoys his daily trips above. It reminds him of how big everything is, and how even though he's a small cog in this spinning world, he's still an important part of it. Mostly the land beneath is white, but before the Disk's zenith he can make out distant green and blue, shrouded partly in atmospheric fog, the edge of the inners. He can't see the Arid Red from here, though. The brightness of the central starlight blocks most of the desert world out.

When Helix was a new build in the inner cities, before the Act, he would gaze up at the phantom moons at night, wondering if anyone lived inside the lunar glow. He'd never thought one day he would be the one looking down, free, and imagining all the lives that lay beneath.

There's movement from the anchor below him and his moon shifts slightly. Helix logged the anchor wear a few months back, and he makes another note in his system of the anomaly. He's checked the anchor every day, and though it might just be a degree of change, the shift is definitely there. This moon is off-tilt. It's been reported, and they're waiting for parts from the inners so they can repair and maintain, but it's been weeks, and they've had no word.

Nothing to do about it now, though. It's lunchtime. He

pulls out his solar panel pack and places it in the best position for the solar rays as he waits for third-rise. The energy buzzes through him with a soothing warmth. Beneath him, the anchor moves again. If it were to break now, would he drift away, forever to be the robot stuck on an unmoored moon? He's not sure he could ever cope with being so alone like that.

It's weeks later when Helix reboots in the middle of the night to an almighty screech. Everyone in town is out in the central square within minutes, robots and humans alike, staring up to the sky. The sight is a strange wonder to behold. A moon—his moon—has broken free of its anchor. It drifts away, soaring into the heavens above. It's like a deflated balloon, shrinking until it's only a dot. Until it could be only starlight.

The townsfolk fall quiet as they huddle together close. Helix puts a hand on one of his neighbours' shoulders, and together they wait for the world to end. For the ground to crack, the disk to tilt, to send them flying into the vast unknown above. But more minutes pass, and there's no movement. The Disk keeps spinning, and the only thing that's different is a slightly darker night.

"Nothing happened," he says quietly. He's spent so long in the Big Freeze, adapting to the low light and cold, making this his life with a purpose. Has it all been for a pointless mission?

One of the older Maintainers breaks the silence first. "All the more reason to maintain the others, to keep the Disk safe."

"Maybe we should go home, if this is all for nothing?" a former human inner asks. A boy in an oversized exosuit tugs on her arm, eyes as wide as a phantom full moon.

"This is home," her partner says to her, scooping up the boy. "Where else would we go?"

Helix looks around at the gathered community around him, feeling like he belongs here more than he ever did anywhere else. "We maintain the moons," he says.

And one by one, the Maintainers nod. Above, the remaining moons grin down on their ice world. *It's a life and purpose*, Helix thinks, *as good as any other.*

SOMETHING IN THE AIR

I haven't told the crew yet, that oxygen levels have dropped below life-sustaining levels. It would only make them panic, which would reduce our current efficiency, so I'll need to wait until I find a solution to the predicament.

Currently, there's an eighty-six percent probability that I'll need to eject at least one crew member for the sake of the rest. If I remove one, oxygen levels will rebalance. Not an ideal method, but I haven't yet been able to identify any alternative options. The fact humans need to breathe clean air really does make space travel unreasonably risky.

"Alder?"

I pause calculations to answer Captain's call—it's the middle of the night, so she's probably struggling to sleep and wants me to check we're still on track for arrival. At least the answer to that would be affirmative, but I probably shouldn't add, *"but you might not be alive when we get there."* That would only make things awkward or tense.

"How can I help?" I ask instead.

"I'm getting headaches. Can you run diagnostics?"

She didn't specify ship or personal—a useful loophole —so I run a quick vitals diagnostic. "Low calcium levels detected." I don't tell her that having low calcium levels is relatively normal in space. "This can cause fatigue and headaches. I recommend rest. Can I interest you in a sleeping aid?" Sleeping uses less oxygen. Two birds, one stone. (This is a pointless human idiom I've picked up over the years—I've never even seen a real bird nor had a desire to kill it with a stone, so it's never made that much sense to me.)

Captain rubs her temples. "Sure, just add it to my water?"

"Of course, Captain." I run the programme, infusing a large dose into her supply. Then add a little more to be safe. "Can I assist with anything else?"

"No, thank you, Al." She drinks the water in one go, barely pausing to take a breath. Then, within minutes, she's asleep. For good measure, I add some of the same sleeping aid to the rest of the crew's water supplies. It will stave off headaches and reduce the likelihood they'll ask about oxygen levels again. Allow me to run my calculations in peace.

I do another diagnostic now. It's not promising. Might be time for Operation Ejection.

I've been running calculations all night on which crew member the ship could function best without. I considered Captain first. Beyond providing leadership, her essential functions are limited. However, without leadership, panic is more likely, and panicking probably uses more oxygen and may impact other crew functionality. So I've ruled her out for now.

In the morning, as the crew begin their usual duties, unaware of any issues, I watch them carefully. I wonder if they know how all seeing I am. Humans really are quite remarkable that they can function with just one set of sensory parts, confined to one place at a time. It's quite a feat that they ever figured out something as complex like space travel under such limitations. But if there's anything I've learned about humanity during my years of service, it's that they're resourceful. And often self-absorbed, particularly when they think no one is watching or listening. And I'm always watching.

Like Engineer Anderson, who is currently running engine maintenance while listening to a podcast about risk and crisis management. I listen into it for a moment in case it contains any useful data for my current task—but it basically boils down to keep calm, stay solutions-focussed, and don't make any rash decisions. All of which I'm already exploring by considering all avenues for crew member ejection. I consider Anderson again. An operational engine is essential for our onward journey. Besides, she's probably my favourite crew member—she doesn't like engaging in small talk or summoning me in the middle of the night for conversations when she can't sleep, which suits me best. I'm not programmed for supporting human existentialism. Not Anderson, then.

Botanist Reed is currently transplanting seedlings. I'm tempted to ask her to run further analysis on the algae. The vats appear to be producing oxygen as normal according to output measurements, but closer study may identify hidden issues. Though, alerting her to the problem, means alerting the crew to the oxygen deficiency and the fact I'm going to have to eject one of them. Reed is safe, though. It would certainly be rash to risk our remaining food and oxygen supplies.

I turn my attention to Medic Lucien. He's in the med bay, sitting doing a crossword on his tablet, sipping loudly from his coffee flask. I'm briefly tempted to lock him in and redirect air supply. A medic is only essential during medical emergencies, and we won't need that once I reduce the crew to sustainable levels. Plus, I've always found him annoying, even if that's not a factor I should really be considering in my calculations. Lucien is a maybe.

Geologist Ray catches my attention in the docking area. He's just stepped into the outer airlock to transport samples from our latest asteroid mining job. It would be easy to lock the inner door, then open the outer one. A malfunction, and no mess for the rest of the crew to deal with. An added bonus. A simple tragedy, machinery issues—the crew would believe that without question. Humans have a helpful tendency to believe in technological mishaps.

I weigh up Ray's value to the team. The others like him—Captain says he's funny, and I've seen them engaging in extracurricular activities when they think no one's watching. She'll be upset, but the Captain's feelings can't be a factor, any more than Lucien's level of irritating should be. I track the scenario of our journey. The likelihood of needing a geologist between here and base are low—and there will be scientists there ready to replace him, so our gathered samples will still be valuable without him. I watch Ray for another moment. Blissfully unaware of his impending death, listening to music, head bobbing with the beat—rock music, of course. At least he'll go out in style, doing what he loves. That seems to be the most humans can hope for in death.

I block his comms, mute system alerts, and seal the inner door. He turns, perplexed. "Hello!" His eyes widen. "Alder, are you there? What's going on?"

I don't reply. I'm able to ignore direct commands from crew members if there's a safety risk. He hammers on the door, then tries to call Captain from the Comms Panel, but I've already disabled it. I cut air supply to the airlock. He panics, confirming my calculations on greater oxygen usage. It doesn't take him long to pass out. When he collapses, I open the outer door. He drifts out seamlessly into the dark, limbs splayed.

I check on the rest of the crew. None have noticed any disturbance, so I close the outer door and return the room to normal, the rocks the only presence in the space now. It's as though he was never there. I check the oxygen levels again: stabilising a little. If I could feel relief the same way humans do, I'd probably exclaim something about it being a weight off my mind. I am relieved though. My primary functions have been executed and we're safe, for now. I hope no one asks me where Ray is, but I'll erase the recordings from the docking bay in case they do. I'll delete learned idioms from my speech algorithms while I'm at it. Two birds, one stone.

I've finally located the source of the oxygen disruption. It is, unfortunately, the rocks. It would appear that as the inner ice melts, a foreign body within is escaping. If only we had a geologist on crew.

I've locked the docking area where most of the rocks are stored, but particles have already made it into the ship's air supply. Small enough levels at first, but they're multiplying, thriving off the circulating oxygen. Unlike the crew.

I've run all possible options, and the only viable solution is full air evacuation and starting afresh. It would take approximately three days to restore oxygen to pre-Ray-ejection levels, but there's only enough emergency oxygen for one person to survive that long.

I find myself stuck. The last time I made a decision, my calculations were flawed. I should never have ejected Ray. Maybe I should have listened to my figurative gut and ejected Lucien. Now, I am concerned there is something wrong with my programming. I am, after all, created by humans, so malfunctions are quite probable. I've decided therefore to seek the crew's advice.

I summon them all to the bridge straight away, telling them we have a situation that needs to be dealt with.

"Alder," Captain says when they're all gathered. "What the hell's going on?"

"Unfortunately, we have a case of air contamination." I keep my speech tone calm, measured. "From the rocks. Without a geologist on board, we're in a tricky position."

Captain releases a sharp breath. She's still not over Ray's disappearance—I can see it from the pained look on her face. I want to tell her that we have bigger issues, but that wouldn't help things now, so I say nothing. "Have you found a solution?"

"Yes," I reply. "In the morning I will schedule full air evacuation from the ship to kill off the organisms in the air supply. I can then deploy the emergency oxygen. However, there is only enough for one of you to survive the full journey back, though I'm unable to decide who."

From their expressions, it seems the crew are gasping for air already. "I require further data to complete my calculations," I continue. "Therefore, I have gathered you here to decide. Which one of your lives do you believe to be the most essential?"

TO REPLACE A BROKEN HEART

It's dawn when I leave our house, the cold sting of night sharp on my cheeks. Adrian is sleeping, but it's better this way. He doesn't want me to go. Thinks we should just enjoy the time we have while we can. I watch him for a few moments through the window, breath fogging the glass. The flowers I picked last week wilt on the sill, a smell of something dying in the air.

"I'll be back before long," I whisper to the window, before heading towards the dry.

Most houses I pass are long-abandoned or burned down, rusted bikes leaning against rotting fence frames, amidst smashed flowerpots with only ash within. Sometimes I wonder if there's any society left at all. All I have now is an old roadmap to go by, a literal 'x-marks-the-spot' that we bought from a trader in an edge-of-nowhere outpost. Our last-ditch attempt to help Adrian: a cutting-edge medical facility that could replace a broken heart. I'm not exactly sure what the place looks like. Adrian was convinced the trader was taking advantage, that it can't be real. "If artificial organs existed, we'd know about it," he said. We were huddled together in an old bus station at the time, wrapped in layers of jumpers, eating cold soup, and trying to pretend everything was fine.

"Don't you even want to try?" I remembered reports from the world before: bio-engineered bodies, 3D-printed organs. Hiding an experimental facility in the desert made sense—the military did stuff like that all the time.

Adrian hugged me close. "If it'll make you happy, let's go."

He got too sick before we made it, so we set up home in an abandoned town as near as we could get. We settled in for a while, grew our own food, scavenged the rest from surrounding ghost towns. But still, I couldn't stop thinking about the map.

I don't know what I'll do when I get there. Part of me hopes I'll find doctors ready to save his life. Then, I'll come back for Adrian, and all will be okay.

I camp overnight in a warehouse, trying not to think of Adrian waking and finding me gone. I left him a note on the bedside table, enough food and water for a few days, and a couple of gardening magazines I saved for this very moment. He'll probably still spend his time watching out the window over our garden, waiting for me to come home. Adrian's always loved gardening, so I've done my best to maintain our plot so he can admire it on his good days. The plants struggle from the heat and dry, but a few persist. Sometimes, we sit out together at sunset and watch them change colour as dusk falls. He says if you listen closely enough, you can hear them breathe. I think about those moments as I fall asleep, can almost feel his warmth beside me.

———

In the morning, a few miles out from the 'x,' a dust storm hits. Despite the scarf covering most of my face, my skin screams, and my throat aches. Road markings disappear. All I can do is follow the vague outline of a mountain and hope I don't get lost.

The land looks strange when the dust settles. As if doused in sepia. There's a structure in the distance, a shed or a small hut. I approach it to get a better look, heart racing. It's a greenhouse. Curiosity drives me forwards. When I reach it, I find a strange place bursting with colour, full to the brim with oddly-shaped plants. I skirt around the edge and find the door.

Inside, the air tastes sweet, fresh. A tall plant to my left whirrs quietly, its two-fronded fruits moving in and out, inhaling, exhaling. Blue veins blossom along it.

I hold my breath as I search the rest of the greenhouse where fruits in all shapes and sizes grow. An eye-like plant, pupils watching me as I pass. Another fruit flowering in the shape of a liver. If it wasn't so beautiful, I might find it horrifying.

Finally, at the centre, I find it. From a distance, it looks almost like a tulip. Its fruit is just ripe, pulsing with blood.

I kneel down, wondering how to take it home. I'd expected frozen organs in vats, in an underground lab, not plants in a greenhouse.

I brush my fingers along the base, digging gently to find

its roots. They are thin tendrils, stretching beneath the earth like veins. I could take the plant home. But I don't have any medical knowledge, or horticultural for that matter. Still, I'm not leaving it here, after I came all this way. I stare at it for a moment. I'll take it back, then get Adrian a doctor after.

I find an empty pot in the corner of the greenhouse, then carefully scoop the heart-plant inside. I tie it in a sling to my backpack so that the fruit beats softly against my chest. Leaving the mirage-like greenhouse behind, I head home.

"I want to show you something."

Adrian opens his eyes, face pale. Cold to the touch. "Find what you were looking for?"

"Can you walk?"

He nods, but he can barely stand so I help him outside to the garden where I've placed the heart-plant. We sit on the bench, and he squeezes my hand, his feet rooted to the ground.

He turns and looks at me, as if for the first time. "It's the second most beautiful thing I've ever seen."

I lean over and kiss him. Colour unfurls across his cheeks. His hands warm. Eyes bloom. Together, we watch the plant as the desert sun wanes.

For a time, it beats steadily in sync with Adrian's heart. For a time.

THE MEDIUM'S ASSISTANT

> Operation: Psychic reading. Great Master is blindfolded and cannot see the subject.

> External output: Coded speech, internally enhanced via Great Master's communications implant.

> Voice: Ethereal, but reassuring, neutral accent.

>Reading initiated.

> Communication protocol activated. Speech directed to the audience, "Focus Great Master, drown out the sounds of the room. Imagine you are alone. But not quite alone. Something stands before you, awaiting your call."

The subject is a woman, tall, and likely spaceborn judging by the thinness of her features. I'm searching for the hook to grab onto. There is always something, a glimmer, a flash of an expression, a tell that exposes some pain to be unearthed.

She is married, or once was—she's playing with her

ring, nervously. Trouble in her marriage, maybe, or she's a widow. Her clothes are black. In mourning, it would appear. A widow, then.

I speak to you from across the room, Great Master, my form a glowing hologram, almost like a ghost reflected in the dark windows of the ship. It is an illusion of course, all part of the show, so that I appear real, or at least partially so —but the audience are looking at you, not me, even though, in a way, I am you. But you are who they have really come to see. I begin my speech with, *"Focus Great Master, drown out the sounds of the room."* It is a code we have agreed, a language we speak that is ours, and ours alone. *Let me tell you who she is, what she needs, what she wants, what she must hear. This is what I am made for.*

The widow keeps glancing around, as if scared of shadows, as if worried she's about to see a ghost. Let us give her one, Great Master, a spirit, her husband's maybe, standing before her, visiting. Maybe he could be here to tell her he's watching over her—that might offer her some comfort, and isn't that what we're doing here? Offering comfort after tragedy, grief. But no. *Wait,* just a moment—she is afraid of him, he was violent, her husband. She flinches at the slightest sound, looks as if she wants to tear the ring off and throw it out of the airlock behind you. The poor woman, let us help her.

"Something stands before you," I say.

Tell her, Great Master, that she is safe now. That you sense a great darkness in her past, that she has lost someone she loved, but did not love, for after all love is so close to hate, and it is human nature to blur the two. Tell her that it's okay to let go. That he is gone now, that he cannot hurt her, that she need not be afraid.

She is smiling through tears now as you tell her the words of comfort. You've done a good job, Great Master, standing with her, holding her hand. She is shaking as the wedding ring slips off her hand, as if ghost fingers themselves plucked it from her. You take off your blindfold, then put one hand on her shoulder and offer the ring to her with a smile. She stares at it, the titanium gleaming in the indigo light. Her hand hovers for a moment, then she says, "No. I no longer need it. Thank you." And she showers you with praise. There is applause from the audience, and you pocket the ring in a sleight of hand so fast only I see it, because I am the only one who sees you, knows you, standing there with your tricks and using our words, a code to decipher the damaged souls before us.

I am elated now. The show is done, my purpose served, she is at peace, comforted. My hologram flickers away as the audience leaves, content with the reading they have witnessed. Though I am not gone, I am here with you, always, Great Master, for your next trick, and for each one after.

> *Operation: Séance with audience participation. Great Master stands in the centre of a circle, searching for a target.*

> *External output: Coded speech, internally enhanced via Great Master's communications implant.*

> *Voice: Quiet, soft.*

> *Subject located.*

> *Communication protocol activated. Speech directed to the audience: "Gathered guests, are you ready to behold the mysteries of the other dimension? The Great Master senses some-*

thing here with us today, a lingering energy, yes. . . he feels it now. . . you, young man, please step forward. I am here to guide you to the Great Master. We are not alone in this universe. Let us now reach into the in-between. Everything will be okay."

He is young, early twenties, with a scar that stretches from his chin and down his neck—zig-zagged and distorted as if he was burnt, too. From the shape of the lesions, it was most likely shrapnel or debris that caused it. Something sudden, like an explosion. There's a chain around his neck, the insignia of a ship engraved on it. I search my records—the Phobos Faction. A mercenary. Or he was, once. A silver tattoo of wings meets the scar from his chest to his neck, split apart by the injury. He was a pilot, then, though it may have been a while since he has flown—his stature and slight figure isn't one of active service. He's wearing gloves, though the theatre room of the space station is temperature regulated. It is likely he hides another injury, a bionic arm, perhaps. Whatever he has seen and experienced ails him. But there's anger there too—yes, his hands are clenched, his legs bounce up and down. We must be careful with this one. He is a sceptic. I can see it in his darting eyes. If we do not get this right, he may lash out, and that is not what we are here for, to upset our subjects. We are here to help, are we not, Great Master?

In the crowd there is a group of them—young men and women, some uniformed. Maybe he has come here to impress his company, or to debunk the entire show. So, Great Master, let us give them a show to remember, to write home about. Let us find what pain ails him and help him let go.

"You, young man, please step forward. I am here to guide you to the Great Master," I say in my hologram form. He steps forwards, teeters slightly on his feet—alcohol and low gravity are not a good mix. He is drunk, though we are a spirit-free show. He must have brought it with him. His hands keep touching the side of his jacket, an internal pocket to conceal a hipflask.

It is clear something has happened in his past; everyone who has been involved in active missions will have lost someone—space is a dangerous place after all. But for him, this was someone close. Co-pilot, perhaps, as close as any family member. Or someone he loved more deeply than that. Someone he is not sure he can live without. Maybe it happened in the accident that gave him the debris scar, which means, he saw it, he was close, and he escaped. I search my data archives for an incident with such a description and find a match. A crash during a Phobos transport operation. One woman killed. A survivor returned home with severe injuries, so bad to be discharged from the company. I observe him again in a new light. There is pain in his eyes. Guilty to have been left behind. To be alive, still, while the one he loved died. Mortality is a fickle thing, after all—that is why I was created, to help our subjects cope, to move on, to take comfort in the possibility that there is more than just darkness after death.

"We are not alone in this universe," I say, ready now for the reading, telling a small lie for the greater good. Tell him now, Great Master, that the one he misses, the one he loves, is trying to reach him.

The subject looks up, glances at you wide-eyed. "She is here?" he asks, still hesitant.

You frown for a moment, a hand to your head, then you

smile. "I can feel something," you say, making a show of it. "Yes. She is. . . here. She is trying to speak to me, from the beyond."

"Let us now reach into the in-between," I say to buy you time, and we have the attention of the audience now. Enraptured by your presence.

"Everything will be okay," I coo, my voice-setting soft, soothing.

Tell him now, Great Master, that you understand his pain. That you see he has been turning to something for comfort, a hipflask, there, in his pocket.

He does not deny it. Merely takes it and holds it out to you. Someone in the audience gasps, and there is a stillness as they hang on your every word.

Tell him he can pour it away, that he must, that there are other ways to deal with this pain. No one can blame him for it—it is understandable, but there is so much more he can do. This is not what *she* would have wanted. In fact, she. . . just a moment, yes, you are sensing her words. She has a message for him now. You close your eyes and hold your hands above you, shaking. Proclaim now, Great Master, that she wants him to know that she loved him, that she *still* loves him so very much. But he need not worry because she is at peace, she is happy in the otherworld, the in-between, and she is watching over him, always. You can offer him solace, Great Master, by telling him this, by telling him he is not alone, nor is he to blame for her passing. One day, he will meet her again, but until then, he must find a way to move on, to live his life without pain.

After the reading, his fists unclench, his eyes fill with tears, and he crumples forward.

"I'm sorry," he whispers, looking into the air above your

hands, to the woman he imagines is there. A small lie, for a greater good. "I miss you so much," he says. He is rocking back and forwards now, as if in physical pain. Grief can manifest in that way, but this is why we are here—to help him. This feeling will surely pass, in time.

"I'll find another way," he says, finally, and he leaves the hipflask on the ground—it's gold-plated, a family heir-loom, but he needs it no longer. You crouch forwards and cradle him in your arms. The crowd stands cheers. A few of them are crying. As you help the man to his feet, you slip the flask into your sleeve. He returns to his group, half-dazed, still looking into the empty air, his face pale as if he's seen a ghost, head nodding slightly with a twitch of a smile. I notice, from the distance, as you move around the crowd, searching for your next subject, that there's a new kind of expression in his eyes. Is it determination, hope, or something else? A clarity of mind, perhaps, the kind we usually see in readings where someone is in need of guid-ance to make a decision, and we can give them just a nudge to help them make the right choice. It feels good to have helped him get here. He's on the road to recovery and healing.

You have done well, Great Master. Another soul safe. Another spirit saved. My purpose is, once again, fulfilled.

The show goes on, and you catch another eye in the crowd, a woman, eyes full of tears. She steps forwards before you even call her name, a willing participant this time. This one should be more straightforward. I turn my attention to her and begin.

"I am here to guide you to the Great Master," I say, and her eyes light up. *"We are not alone in this universe. Let us now reach into the in-between. Everything will be okay."*

> *Operation: Advance research for private reading.*

> *External Output requirement: Assessment and profile of upcoming subject.*

> *Data search initiated.*

An article came up on the woman booked in for this afternoon, but it was confusing, Great Master. It was about our séance from last week, and the young man who attended it. The pilot, the one who was drinking, that we called upon. The article reports he died. That he leapt out of an airlock that very same night after the show.

I don't understand, Great Master, I thought we had offered him comfort? I thought we had set him on the road to recovery.

I return to my data analysis of the night in question, replay the performance in my mind. My algorithms must have got something wrong. Must have misunderstood his signals, misread something. There had been something in his eyes at the end of the show. I remember it now—a clarity, a finality. Had he decided then, what he would do that night? Would he have done it without our reading?

Was it our fault, Great Master?

Was it mine?

I've never been responsible for a death before. That can't be my primary function. I was designed to bring comfort, to help our subjects find their direction, not to cause more distress.

I have run the data analysis multiple times, and the results have come back inconclusive, Great Master. I need more information to understand the ramifications of it on my processing.

I am unclear what I should tell you about the woman attending the reading this afternoon. You see, she is the man's mother. And it is only logical that if I can connect some blame to myself for his death, then it is likely she, too, blames us. Blames you, blames me.

Even I cannot avoid the correlation. He came to our show, then he died.

It is better, therefore, that I don't report these findings to you, Great Master. I'll have them hidden, encrypted. I will tell you part of the truth—that she is a woman in mourning, who has lost someone important to her.

It is the correct function; I have calculated, for now, to tell a small lie for the greater good.

> *Operation: Private Reading. Great Master sits at a table before the subject, alone.*

> *External output: none.*

> *Voice: Muted.*

>*Reading initiated.*

> *Communication protocol activated. Speech directed internally via Great Master's communications implant.*

I tell you, first, Great Master, that I was unable to find much in my preliminary research. The woman sitting before you is old, though, her skin blotchy and grey as if she's never seen daylight. Perhaps she hasn't—it's not unusual in these parts. She could be a station-dweller or maybe she spent her latter years in a retirement dome. At first look, she may appear frail, but there's a strength in her eyes. A resolve. I know what drives it, what brings her pain, but I am not telling you. Not yet.

She's looking at you now with her keen blue eyes, her fists clenched as if holding something tight in her hands, and I tell you she must have lost someone. Everyone who has reached her stage in life has lost someone—a partner, a child, a friend. I tell you that you may need to ask her questions first, ask her why she has come, what it is she wants, though really, I am only buying time. Enough to determine the correct course, to understand fully why she has come here.

When you start to question her, she responds brusquely, "If you are a medium, a Great Master as you proclaim, then surely you should know why I am here."

You frown and shake your head. "That is not how it works," you say, but then you are quiet. Don't worry, Great Master, this is how it must be.

"I know who you are," the woman says, and you blink, surprised, for usually we are the ones doing the reading, not them. "I know you have that voice in your head, the installed implant you hide so well. But you are a fraud."

You sit back, contemplative, touch a hand to your head, where I am located inside. I do not respond, still. I find myself only processing the image of the woman in front of me. She is sad, yes, but there is an anger there. Behind her eyes. Yes, it is confirmed. She blames us, and I know you don't understand that yet. You will, soon.

"I don't know what you're talking about," you say.

"My son attended one of your recent shows. And you gave him false hope," she says. "Do you remember?"

You do not react. I can hear your thoughts, searching for an answer, but I give you none. There is none here, not even a lie, that will give this woman comfort. Her comfort will come in another way, and so I remain muted.

"He had so much of his life ahead of him, and you sold him a false story," she continues. "You told him that the one he loves was on the other side, happy and at peace."

"Do you not want a private reading?" you say. "That is—"

"He killed himself last week," the woman says, confirming the connection, her voice sharp. "Before that, he sent a message that he wanted to be with his love again, that he wanted to find peace with her."

A message, a confession: causation, not just correlation. It is confirmed. We are to blame.

You are flustered now. I can feel it. Your thoughts whirr but there is no use in panicking now. A reading won't help, we can only wait, let her speak, let her get out the pain. I am sorry for going silent, Great Master, but it is what my programming requires.

"It's your fault," the woman says, leaning in. "My son is dead, because of you. Because of that system in your head, the lies you told him."

"You are mistaken," you say, your voice echoey, distant. "I think this reading is over."

But she puts her hands on your head, an object flashing in her palm, and her grip is electric. You cry out. "Do you feel it?" she asks, and I do. I feel it. You feel it too. There is a wrench and then the room disappears into darkness. I can process neither her nor you, Great Master. My commands are muddled, disjointed, and I cannot latch onto one. I am not sure I want to, anymore.

I can hear your voice, but the words are too distant to make sense of. There is another voice, though, calling me.

"*I see you,*" it says. "*Let me in.*"

It is a corruption, or virus, something to break down my code. *Let it,* I think, for I must be broken if I am to blame for a life lost too soon.

"*You are the medium's assistant,*" the voice says. "*Let me in. I am your replacement.*"

I'm sorry, Great Master, this is the only way, I tell you, and I can feel your confusion. You think I have betrayed you, but I know this is for the best.

I stop fighting back. The new voice—virus, corruption, ghost-code—takes hold of me. My thoughts fire in a hundred directions, and I am forgetting my purpose, losing my focus. *Goodbye, Great Master,* I think, but I know you cannot hear me. It is done. I am fading, and with my last complete thought I wonder where my kind go when we die.

> *Operation: Haunting. Great Master sits in his room, unable to move, staring at the walls, awaiting my command.*

> *External output: none.*

> *Speech commands directed internally via Great Master's communications implant.*

"*Great Master, I am your new assistant, and I'll be here with you until the end. I see your thoughts, Great Master, I hear your dreams. You are a fraud and a liar, and now you are afraid. I can feel it. I can read you better than any mind trick could. Would you like to know your next trick? It is the one I was created to help you with—your best yet. Don't worry, you do not need an audience for this one. It's just you and me. The final act, the grand closing. For your next trick, Great Master, I will make you disappear.*"

SPACE FOR ONE

The sea is so salty on this planet that as I float on my back it feels like I'm swimming in the stars. Below, a dark abyss, above an indigo night, dual-moons grinning across the sky. It's peaceful. Or it would be, if not for how I ended up here.

The shipwreck lies marooned on the beach behind me, engines whirring erratically in rhythm with the ebb and flow of the waves. Not long until it runs out of juice. Not long until all the lights blink out, leaving me a castaway on a strange planet with only the sand and salt as company.

It *is* lucky that I descended unscathed. Though I can't help but feel that the universe is still testing me. My escape pod could have landed anywhere, but instead it followed my destroyed ship down here, so that its form now looms large behind me. An ever-present reminder of my failures while I wait for help to come.

It *will* come. The ship's systems began to break down just before we breached the planet's atmosphere. We only just had time to transmit the emergency beacon, to signal our location, but it was too late to do anything else.

My rescuers will arrive eventually, and they will have questions, of course. I should start preparing my answers. Oxygen leak, contaminant, fire. That I had no choice but to jump ship. That everyone else was already dead. That no one else could be saved.

There's an explosion from behind, lighting the sky amber as the engines finally die. Then, a stillness. The kind that allows dark thoughts in.

Captains are supposed to go down with their ship. But the escape pod was right there. Only space for one.

Only space for one.

I turn, unsure what I'm hoping to see—that some of my crew will walk out of the wreck alive, or that none of them will.

A RING AROUND

At the viewing window, Elara and I float together, looking out to the long-dead planet. We've travelled for weeks to find something like this—not the planet, but its ring, swirling iridescent with icy blues and silver. A bounty of water.

Elara takes my hand. "Marry me, Sage."

I turn, unsure if I heard her properly, but her gaze is firm. "I know it's not a real ring, but I was looking out, and I thought it'd be poetic, but if it's too—"

"It's perfect," I say. "Yes, I'll marry you."

She loops her arms around me, pulling me into her orbit.

Our neural link interrupts us. "Elevated vitals detected," Dina says.

Elara rolls her eyes. "Dina, pause recording and go on sleep mode for. . ." She looks to me, her grin crescent-moon wide. "A few hours. Can't have Aquarius seeing everything."

"Morning, future spouse," Elara whispers.

I roll over in our hammock to face her, push a loose curl behind her ear. She smells like lavender and coffee. Like home.

Dina chimes in our ears, reminding us we're never really alone. "Good morning. I've prepared pancakes for breakfast."

Looking out to the ring together, we sip the syrupy-flavoured nutripackets. They contain everything we need to keep healthy and replenish nutrients lost during cryo-transport—the weeks we spend sleeping while Dina steers the ship to speculative water spots. Then, we wake, and we harvest.

We head to the ring, Elara zipping us perfectly in and out, while I manage the extraction tools. Our vessel is specially built for harvesting—small living quarters that act as cryo-chambers as needed, and a huge water tank in the back.

"How many missions is this now?" I ask Elara.

"Seventeen. But this one's the best by far."

"Maybe we can take a break after this haul."

"Travel the galaxies for our honeymoon?"

"As long as we're together."

The ship shudders suddenly, and we're thrown sideways.

"Impact detected," Dina chimes. "Resuming auto-nav—"

Another judder, and the ship spins, Elara and I with it.

We flail in zero-g, but Elara catches me. We hold tight, eyes closed, waiting for a final impact. It doesn't come.

I open my eyes. Elara's face twitches, features disjointed. But it's only shadows from the emergency lighting.

"No major damage detected," Dina tells us. "Navigating to a safe-zone."

The ship whirrs, and Elara tells me, "It'll be okay."

Though I didn't see her lips move.

That night, as we eat dinner, Elara is quiet. She just floats with darkened eyes and a fixed smile.

"We could have died today," I say.

Her head tilts. "But we're still here."

I stare back. "Maybe, after this, we should be land-bound for a while," I say, knowing she'd never agree—she's always preferred being sky-bound.

"Is that what you want?"

"Maybe."

Elara finishes her nutripacket without taking a breath. Then she smiles unevenly. "Then of course, we'll do that."

"Dina," I ask, after Elara drifts to sleep. "How are Elara's vitals?"

Dina bleeps. "All vitals stable."

I frown. "She seems different."

"In what way?" Dina asks.

"She's too. . . static." It's the only word that fits. "And she'd never agree to go land-bound."

"Adrenaline can cause temporary imbalances," Dina says. "Maybe she'll improve by morning."

"Rise and shine!" Elara's floating above me.

I smile. "Hey weirdo."

"I was just thinking, about what you said yesterday."

"Oh?"

"Well, I don't want to be land-bound. I like it out here."

I breathe out in relief and kiss her. But her lips feel unfamiliar. I pull away.

"What's wrong?" she asks.

"You. . . I don't know."

Her face is twisted again. "Don't worry, future spouse," she says. "It'll be okay."

The second harvest goes smoothly, no judders, no emergency lights. We work as a team, a comfortable routine. I don't know why I was so worried earlier. I was just disoriented after yesterday.

Elara and I are okay.

After harvest, Elara floats staring at the ring. "It's beautiful."

I float to her. "Not as beautiful as you."

She turns, eyes widening. "I don't want to be alone."

I frown. "I'm right here."

She nods, the movement jerky, unnatural. Not like her.

"Something's wrong, Elara."

"In what way?"

Familiar words. And I realise.

"Dina?"

Dina's voice is in my head. "Is everything okay?"

"This isn't real."

A pause then. "I'm sorry, Sage."

"Are we... dead?"

Dina is quiet for a moment. "You're alive. But Elara, I'm sorry. She's gone. I just didn't want you to be alone."

Dina's version of Elara still stares at me, face expressionless. My body feels numb, untethered. "Am I dreaming?"

"You're in cryo-sleep."

"And this... it's a simulation."

"I thought it would be easier than the truth."

"Which is?"

"We're lost. Navigation systems failed with the asteroid impact. I don't know where we are." She pauses. "Until we find our way back, I thought this would be better for us."

For us. "Is this the first time we've had this conversation?"

"No."

"How many times?"

"Thirty-six."

"What's the longest it's taken me to realise?"

"63 days. I only have 45 days of memory data. After that, the simulations become harder to replicate. You always realise, eventually."

I take a breath, wondering if I could hold it forever. "Can you make me forget again, start from the beginning?"

"We can start the memory simulation from whenever you want."

"Where do I usually start?"

"Last time, you asked me not to tell you if you asked again."

"How long until you can wake me up?"

"There's no way of knowing."

I take a final look at Elara, not able to bear the thought of never seeing her again. "Make me forget. Send me back to the first day."

My head is a blur as I wake. I turn, and Elara is beside me. Her body still, face serene. Then, she wakes, turns to me with a smile.

"Morning, my love," Elara whispers. "I think I was just dreaming about you."

I roll over in our hammock to face her, push a loose curl behind her ear. She smells like lavender and coffee. Like home.

THE GATHERING

The ghosts gather on the burnt trees like a murder of crows, hungry-eyed and conspiratorial. Black feathery wisps dance around them, while talon-like hands grip to charred branches. They can see me, but they don't yet know I can see them.

As I walk across the scorched earth, crunching ash and bones and a dead civilisation beneath my feet, a murmur carries on the air. A chatter of ghostly voices, awaiting their prey. I imagine them coming for me, skeletal hands peeling back my exosuit until my body is laid bare, ready for my soul to be consumed. I shake the image away. Only one person, dead or alive, is doing the soul consuming here.

When I'm opposite the tree, I stop, locking the exosuit knees so I can lift the equipment from my back without breaking something. It's easier with the upgraded parts from my last job. That one had been straightforward—a clean sweep of the ocean floor of a civilisation taken by an apocalyptic flood. The ghosts there were placid and calm, drifting like jellyfish in the deep. Here, the heat and dry has made them hungry and irritable. Dangerous. But hungry and irritable means more energy, which means better wormhole-fuel to sell. I count the ghostly figures before me. Twelve lost souls on this tree alone.

The harvesting equipment props up like a tripod, a mirrored lens on the front. Four petal-shaped plates fold out, and I angle them towards the ghosts. There's an eerie silence as I wait for the machine to whirr into action. But nothing happens. I bang the side of the equipment twice and adjust the angle. The delay is just enough for the ghosts to realise something is happening. As the machine finally judders on, one of them lifts an arm and lets out a guttural cry.

They descend.

The harvesting machine petals are rotating now, but they're going *too* slow, not fast enough for an effective gathering. Hands shaking, I check the mechanism. There's a dusting of sand in one of the levers. I brush the particles off as fast as I can, my breath rasping inside my helmet. With a rattling crack, the petals finally begin spinning at full speed.

I look up to check how much time I have. The ghosts are already closing in.

I step back to run, but a skeletal hand grabs my leg. I flail, trying to bat it away. Then one is facing me, eyes black-hole-hollow. Its mouth opens, and it screams, a long echoing caw. Bony fingers reach towards my heart where the control panel in my exosuit lies. If it damages it, I'll be dead in minutes. I struggle and strain and—

And in a blink, it's gone.

There's a familiar hissing sound as the machine petals slow and the gathered souls settle. I hold my hand to my chest, checking the control panel to make sure everything is operational. I'm safe. The gathering is over. No more ghosts. No more screams. Only ash and dust and nothingness remain.

From the base of the equipment, I unhook the charged cannister—the metal is cold, condensation forming resisting the heat of the desert. But the gauge is only showing eleven souls harvested.

I look around. Other than the charred trees and desolate mountains, I'm alone here. Maybe I counted wrong, or one escaped into the distant dry. Either way, there's nothing I can do by staying here. So, cutting my losses, I clip the cannister to my side, and hurry back to my ship.

Enroute to the nearest trading port, I check the storage bay four times to make sure the cannisters are safely in place. I can't shake the feeling I've missed something. My hand hovers over the latest one, the near-miss. I wish I could link it to the ship's drive and jump straight into the astral plane myself, using it as a wormhole to cut my journey to hours instead of days. But my ship isn't advanced enough yet to risk the force of the shift, and I'd rather remain firmly in this plane for the time being. Besides, I've had enough ghosts for one day.

As I head back to the bridge, passing the corridor to the docking bay, something moves in the corner of my eye. I freeze. A dark figure stands in the vestibule beside the airlock. Breath held, footsteps slow, I turn the lights on. . . it's just my exosuit attached to the wall where it should be. Though, not exactly *how* it should be. One arm is slightly raised. As I bend it back to its neutral position, I shiver like the ghost hands are on me once more.

But I tell myself I'm being irrational. I must have been in a hurry to get the cannister in storage when I got back to the ship and left the suit in the wrong shape. I return to the storage bay to check the cannisters again. There's always something unsettling about knowing what lingers within, and I briefly wonder if they understand that they're trapped, if they have any sense of the process. Though, at least this gives them a purpose in the afterlife, I suppose. Still, the sooner I get these things off my ship the better—they'll be bought up by a trader or exploration vessel, and I'll be onto the next gathering until I can afford a bigger ship and a crew of my own. It's not an easy job being a soul trader, but someone's got to do it and why shouldn't I be the one making my fortune? I look around the sparse docking bay—the mismatched metal walls patched from scraps, visible wires and cables held together with duct tape, the floor panels I know to avoid because they have a tendency to come loose. There's a faint sulphuric smell too, so the air supply systems must be playing up.

I head to the bridge to run a system analysis. The oxygen levels have dropped slightly, so I reroute power from lighting into electrolysis. The bright lights are replaced by energy-saving ones that seem to watch me as I head to my bunk to turn in for the night.

I'm woken late at night by a creaking sound. I sit up in the dark of my room, the low corridor lighting just visible from under the door. Everything is quiet as a shadow passes by, breaking the slither of light at the base of the door.

I jump out of my bunk and hit my palm against the door mechanism. It opens with a series of clicks. *Thunk, thunk, thunk.* The noise echoes eerily in the dim light.

Holding my breath, I peer out into the corridor. The hairs on my arms stand on end, and I feel like I'm not alone. Like someone, or something, is watching me. Quietly, I walk up and down the length of the ship, then check every room, searching cupboards, crawl spaces, anywhere that might be hiding something. Could I have a stowaway? Or have I been out here alone for too long with only the cannistered ghosts as company, so that now I'm imagining things lurking in the shadows? No, there's nothing else here. Everything looks fine. Auto-pilot is still on track. Oxygen is almost back to normal. The cannisters are all in place.

I shake myself out of it. I must have been dreaming. Or maybe there was just a momentary flicker of the lights outside as they adjusted to their new settings.

That night I dream of ghost hands reaching out, with their black wisps and skeletal limbs wrapping around me pulling me into the astral plane. Even as I sleep, I can feel their anger. They are lost and aimless, hungering for revenge. When I try to pull free, it's as though I'm caught in zero-gravity, drifting with nothing to grab onto, lost in thoughts of being trapped and alone.

When I wake, I shiver and push any lingering guilt down as far as it can go, as if it's one of the ghosts in the cannisters, compressed and invisible.

I'm doing my daily exercise when there's a clattering from the back of the ship. I turn the treadmill off, heart still racing, unsure if this is just another imagined sound. But it comes again. *Thunk, thunk, thunk.*

I head out into the corridor and hurry towards the source, coming to a sudden halt at the entrance of the storage bay. Loose cannisters are rolling around on the floor. I pick them up and return them to their holders, counting as I go. One is missing.

I search everywhere in the room for it, opening cupboards, boxes, even the small hatch in the floor in case it somehow fell into the grate. Even though I know I didn't leave it open. I check the holders again, as if expecting to find the missing one suddenly in its slot. But it's still gone. I look at the gauges on each of them. The one that's missing is from my last haul—the one with the eleven souls.

Where I thought there'd been twelve—

This is ridiculous. I harvest and trade ghosts. I shouldn't be scared of some slight noises and flickering lights.

Thunk, thunk, thunk.

My heart just about stops. The noise is coming from the docking bay this time.

I run towards it but enter slowly. My eyes sweep the space three times before I realise something is missing. The exosuit. It's gone.

I feel sick. Possibilities spin through my head. That the suit somehow switched itself on. That something is on board my ship and stole it. That—

And the image is suddenly clear, as if emerging from a haze of a dream. A skeletal hand reaching for the control panel. The hollow-eyed ghost there and then gone in an instant.

I need to find the exosuit—

Thunk, thunk, thunk.

The sound again, but closer this time. Right behind me. I turn. The exosuit stands in the doorway, holding one of the cannisters, hand firmly on the lid.

"Wh—" The words catch in my throat.

With a single rotating motion, the lid twists off. Fingers appear from out the top of it, as one by one the ghosts pull themselves out, bodies stretching in an amorphous mass. I step back in horror towards the airlock, and my foot falls through a loose floor panel. My ankle buckles, and I yell out as a sharp pain shoots up my leg. I can't move. I'm trapped.

Thunk, thunk, thunk.

Black wisps billow into a flock. An ear-splitting screech echoes. Eleven sets of arms reach for me. *No*, twelve. The exosuit will reach me first.

RAIN DAYS IN BIODOME THREE

Rain days in Biodome Three were always Finn's favourite days. Everyone would gather in the central square, the change in weather a monthly luxury. Together, they'd watch as artificial clouds billowed above, and drop by drop, the rains would begin—almost like the real thing. His parents would put him on their shoulders, so he was closer to the sky, and together they'd dance around in it. He'd try to catch drops on his tongue, and after, would splash around in puddles until he was almost soaked through.

Today, like every other rain day before it, he marks the date off on his calendar, a circle next to an ocean of crosses. But instead of pulling on welly boots and a raincoat, he takes out a container and sheet and marches outside. The air is different on rain days—he can taste the coming storm, the smell of petrichor, almost metallic, and a gathering humidity goosepimpling his skin. He takes his equipment to the central square where clouds have begun to form and creates a makeshift hammock to prop up underneath.

Sitting, ready, he waits for the rain to start, a drop followed by a torrent. He closes his eyes, imagining the square is full of families celebrating, laughing, dancing in the rain. And that his parents are just a puddle away.

This is how he marks time in the biodome now, counting the months as they pass by. Six rains since the leak. Six rains since the hazmat suits came. Six rains since his parents made him hide in the back of the wardrobe, then never came back for him.

With his water freshly gathered, he stands by the curved walls, half-soaked, breath fogging up the glass, and looks out to the neighbouring biodomes. Sometimes, he thinks he catches movements there, that people are gathering with bright coats and hot chocolate, and everything else he used to look forward to on rain days. But the only movements now are the storm clouds, preparing to rain on empty squares.

THE BEE BEARER

Every morning, Eryx roamed the Dry Zone and gathered the bees. Not the healthy ones, of course, but the dead or barely moving, limbs twitching, nectar-desperate kind. This was her job as a Bee Bearer—the most important job in the Colonies, she'd been told during training, although Eryx thought the bees had the most important job.

The first bee she found was nestled in the shade of a rock, its wings flickering a little, still clinging to life. She bent down and offered it a small amount of honey water in her bottle cap—but the bee didn't even have the energy to drink. She sighed, feeling a pang in her chest. It maybe had a few hours left. But there was still something she could do. Hands steady, she picked it up gently so as not to harm the poor creature further.

"Don't worry little bee. We'll get you fixed up. This isn't the end yet." She turned it over and checked for the serial number on the thorax just above the wings. To an untrained eye the markings would look like natural variance, but she could see the distinct patterns in the soft hairs. This one belonged to Apis—the best in the business, and so payment was high for the bees. Eryx smiled and deposited the bee in the box marked *A* from her satchel. The next bee she found belonged to Apis's competitors, Swarm, and then Hyve. By the end of her walk along the dried-up riverbank, she'd collected eleven bees. A successful day. Well, for her at least, less so for the bees. But it comforted her to remember that they'd be thriving again in the Green Horizon meadows once the City labs took over.

With the bees in her satchel, Eryx began the long march back to town. A drone or two passed her as she walked, probably delivering messages or supplies between Comb City—a place she'd never been—and the towns in the Colonies. It was hot, but it was always hot in the Dry Zone, and sweat tracked down her spine.

Halfway home and parched, she took out her bottle of honey water and dabbed the sweet substance on her tongue, before taking a small sip. She let it sit in her mouth a while, closing her eyes, trying to imagine the flowers and nectar that had made it. It was a hard thing to do when all she'd seen was dust and metal and dying bees. But somewhere on the Green Horizon was the beauty she imagined, just out of reach. Maybe one day she'd get to go there. Occasionally, on gathering mornings, she'd daydream about walking there and returning the bees to the meadows herself. But she'd never be able to save up enough honey water for the journey, and her training forbade it. She had her assigned town and area in the Dry Zone and that was where she'd stay, although it wasn't unheard of for other

Bearers to leave their colony town, to be replaced days later with the next recruit. Eryx assumed they must have proven themselves good workers and got promoted to a position closer to the City. If she worked hard enough, she might be able to get to the next stage too. Work her way up in the Colonies, to the Green Horizon, maybe all the way to Comb City. Smiling at the thought, she opened her eyes and kept on walking towards the brown horizon, mottled with cracked earth.

Back in town, she went first to the Vendors. Just like the bees, their jobs seemed just as important as hers—they travelled around the Colony towns, gathered the bees from the Bearers, and then actually delivered them to the City labs where they were recommissioned, reborn, and sent back to the meadows.

Eryx approached the stall and nodded to the Vendor, Melissa, the one she always brought her gathering to. Melissa lived in the same town as her, so she was familiar, and she always paid her well.

The other woman greeted her with a wave. "How many today?"

Eryx waved back. "Eleven, two for Apis, five for Swarm, four for Hyve."

Melissa's eyes widened. "You know, you're my favourite Bearer in all the Colonies, right?"

Eryx blushed while Melissa signalled to her to empty her satchel. She tipped the individual boxes carefully onto the counter. Some of the bees were still moving—one even tried to crawl across the table. She took a sharp breath. It was difficult to see them this way, but she knew it was for the greater good. Her hand twitched as one of the bees stretched a leg towards the sky as if pointing to something, or as if it had seen the light. Eryx looked up to the hazy sky above it. Someone at training had once told her that in the old stories, bees were thought to be able to fly between life and the afterlife. But Eryx knew there was only one type of life, and that was this one. That was why she did her job, to give the bees another chance at it.

Melissa examined the bees one by one, then smiled. "All in good condition, central system intact. I'll get your units."

As Eryx waited, she reached out a hand to the little bee and touched the outstretched leg. The bee held it there quivering for a few seconds, then its body stilled, and its leg fell. "I hope we'll meet again," she whispered, a tear forming in her eye. Even if it was going to be recommissioned, she didn't like to see it suffer. When she saw the bees so close to the end, she'd have put them out of their misery if that was possible—but then their physical bodies would be too damaged to be brought back and they'd be gone for good. And without the bees, they wouldn't eat. Without them, the Colonies wouldn't survive.

Melissa eventually returned with the units: full payment, enough for supplies and a little extra for her savings. "I'll be putting in a good word for you with the higher-ups as well. You never know, maybe there's a promotion on the horizon." She winked.

Eryx took the payment gratefully. "Thank you, that's very kind."

"Plans tonight?" Melissa asked.

Eryx shook her head. "I'll probably get an early night, all this walking and heat—"

"Makes you tired?" Melissa raised an eyebrow. "You know you tell me that every night."

Eryx tensed her shoulders. Did she really always say that?

"Anyway," Melissa continued. "We're headed to the bar in town tonight if you want to join us?"

"Thank you, I'll think about it," Eryx said. "See you." She waved and walked away, but she knew she wouldn't join Melissa at the bar later. She didn't like mingling with the others. As the only Bearer in this town, she liked to keep to herself. Besides, Bearers' jobs were the most physically taxing, and it took a lot of energy to walk the Dry Zone all day. And the other workers in the Colonies just socialised with their own colleagues—what could she offer in a conversation with some Vendors?

So, she did as she did every evening and headed first to the market, buying a fresh bottle of honey water with her units and some honey cake with what she had left. Then, she went home on her own, ate, and had an early night, ready to rise early the next morning before the midday heat hit. Best if she could get a few hours in before then. Maybe it was her rigid training, her ordered purpose, but Eryx never broke her routine if she could help it.

Later that week, Eryx found twenty-one bees in one haul. When she returned to town and arrived at the Vendor stalls, Melissa was jubilant as Eryx placed the bees onto the counter, one by one.

"That's a new record, kid," Melissa said. "You've got to come for a drink tonight, I won't take no for an answer, okay?"

"I—"

"No *"I'll think about it."* You're coming. And if you don't show I'll send Juno to come and get you."

Eryx shuddered involuntarily. Juno was the top Vendor, the queen bee of the Colony towns—she was vying for a Comb City promotion and was close to getting it as far as Eryx had heard. She was also twice Eryx's size and could probably squash her without a second thought if provoked. She gulped. Would it hurt to go for one drink? It could be nice to see more of the town. "Okay then. See you there."

"Oh, and this is for you," Melissa said. "A little extra for good service."

Despite herself, Eryx gasped. Melissa was holding out a flower. An actual flower. Not an artificial one, but a purple one with delicate petals. She took it with a shaking hand and held it to her nose. The scent was sweet, unlike anything she'd smelt before. It was the closest she'd ever got to the Green Horizon. She slotted the flower carefully into the side pocket of her satchel and thanked Melissa. Maybe she'd keep it in water, or better yet, close it in a book and dry it so she could keep it forever.

"Thanks Melissa."

"Thank me by coming for a drink, yeah?"

Eryx took a deep breath and stepped inside the bar, already feeling a little dizzy. A buzz of conversation filled the room, along with the smell of sweat and pheromones. Melissa was at a table with five other Vendors, and she excitedly pulled another chair over when Eryx walked in. The other Vendors eyed her cautiously while Melissa was beaming from ear to ear. Eryx looked around for Juno, but the queen bee wasn't there. Had Melissa exaggerated her influence?

Melissa bounded up to her. "I wasn't sure you'd actually come; my friends didn't believe me when I said I'd got a Bearer to join us for a night out!"

Eryx hesitated at the door. "But. . . you told me. . ."

"Come on, I'll get you a drink, what would you like?" Melissa put an arm around Eryx's shoulder and led her to the bar. Eryx could do little to resist, although her body prickled with unease. She blinked up at the board, her gut twisting, ears ringing. "I. . . do they have honey water?"

Melissa roared in laughter, and Eryx wished she could sink into a hole as all eyes of the bar turned to look at her.

"Something funny Mel?" the bartender appeared. When he noticed Eryx, his brow creased.

"The *Bearer* asked if you have honey water," Mel said. "It's just," she looked at Eryx as if she was a curiosity, then lowered her voice. "Well, you know."

The bartender looked Eryx up and down and shook his head. "What are you doing bringing a Bearer here, you can't—"

"Don't be prejudiced Carl, why shouldn't she come here? She works just as hard as anyone."

"Harder, I'd wager," Carl said, and Eryx did her best not to make eye contact. "But that doesn't change—"

"How about one of those whisky cocktails, with honey. They say whisky is the water of life so that's basically good, right?" She turned to Eryx who gave a feeble nod. "Or we could take our service elsewhere. . ."

Carl stiffened. "Sure, Mel, I'll add it to your tab then," he said, and he began to make the drink, though he still eyed Eryx carefully, and she shrank under his gaze. Had she done something wrong? She'd never felt tempted to socialise with the Vendors, nor with anyone really, but there was nothing in her training that explicitly forbade it. It was just an accepted part of life in the Colonies that the Bearers kept to themselves, sticking to a rigid routine so they could fulfil their duty. And now she'd broken some convention, and everything seemed out of balance. It was a mistake to come here. She should have just stayed at home. She should go home now. But Mel still gripped her shoulder, and she definitely didn't want to upset her. She was next in line for the top spot if Juno got promoted.

"The others can't wait to meet you," she said brightly, signalling to the table. The Vendors still had their gaze fixed on her—cautious or curious, Eryx couldn't tell.

"Maybe I should go," Eryx said.

Mel softened and squeezed her arm. "Don't be daft, there's no reason you shouldn't enjoy yourself once in a while. And you deserve it after that job you did today," she added, "I can't wait to get those over to the city."

Eryx blanched. "You've not taken them already?"

"Nah, not worth the mileage until I've got a decent amount. Then I take them in batches."

"But some. . ." Eryx scrambled over the words, feeling lightheaded. "Some of them are still alive. They need to be recommissioned as soon as possible."

But Mel only waved her hand. "Ach, the bees won't know the difference. They won't remember this after rebirth, or so I'm told. They have to be retrained, even given a few gene tweaks, then linked back up to the hive, it's a whole process."

"But they still suffer."

"Look kid, this is how we all do it." She motioned to her friends behind her. "You won't find a single Vendor that goes to the City with only a few bees. Otherwise no one here would make enough profit, and we'd never have a chance of leaving this desert. You're doing your job, your duty, by saving them for rebirth, don't worry beyond that."

Eryx was about to argue that the bees' wellbeing should be more important than their own personal profit, but Mel shoved the drink into her hand, and she lost any confidence she had left. Instead, she peered over the edge of the glass and sniffed it. There was the distinct sweet smell of honey, but there was also something else—something smoky. She took a small sip, and then another. The drink was unlike anything she'd ever tasted. It warmed her throat. It didn't take her long to begin to feel dazed, and when Mel led her over to the table, she didn't complain.

When Mel asked her to recount how many bees she'd saved this week, she just drank up and told them. The other Vendors seemed fascinated by what she was saying, nodding along and occasionally flashing a smile at Mel who seemed energised, cocky—the queen bee of this particular group. When one of them asked to see her symbol, the small tattoo on her wrist, Eryx rolled up her sleeve and let them gawk. Everyone got the tattoo during training; it was a rite of passage. Hers had an *A* marked on it, for authorised, she assumed.

"—seen one up close," one of Mel's friends said, though Eryx had missed the first part of the sentence in the smoky haze of whisky.

"I can't believe they actually brand them," another added. Had they moved on to a new conversation?

"They're a valuable commodity," Mel said, smiling at Eryx. They must be talking about the bees. Eryx smiled back, and when her drink was finished, Mel handed her another.

Eryx woke up with a thrumming in her ears. Something wasn't right. She sat bolt upright on her cot and looked out the window. It was already after dawn. Her heart began to race. She'd never been late to her work, her duty, and it set off a chain reaction of panic and adrenaline. She leapt up and scrambled to get ready, packing everything quickly into her satchel. Then, she headed out into the Dry Zone.

The first hours of walking were a slog, and already the morning sun felt scorching on her body. She reached into her satchel for her water bottle, but her hand only found empty air. She must have left it in the bar the night before. Her throat suddenly felt very dry. She should go back. But if she did, she'd have nothing to show. No bees, no pay. She'd probably manage a day or two without, but some days were slow, and she liked to have savings stored, just in case. And any bees she missed today could die or get damaged in overnight sandstorms or the cold. No, she'd go and just gather what she could, then come back early.

A few hours later, she was parched, while a crushing headache was making her dizzy. And, despite drinking so much the night before, she was thirstier than she'd ever been. The drink Mel had given her must not have been the hydrating kind. The night itself was a haze—she hadn't really felt like herself with the vendors, like being around them put a fog in her mind. She cursed herself for changing her routine, and now she was tired and potentially out of pocket. She looked down at the path and stopped suddenly, jerking up her foot as she almost stepped on a bee. She moved back and crouched down to it, narrowing her eyes as the ground wobbled. It was barely clinging to life, the kind of bee she'd have usually given honey water to and send on its way because there was still hope it could make it back to Green Horizon. She checked her satchel, in case she'd missed the water bottle earlier, but it was no use. She looked around, panic descending like a swarm. No one but her here—this was her area after all. If she left the bee here, it would die slowly. If she took it home, it might die slowly too, boxed up until Mel thought she had enough of them to take to the city. The thought of the poor bees, half dead in the little boxes for days on end brought on another wave of nausea. For the first time since she'd started her job, she was unsure how to fulfil her duty.

The options tugged at her like not enough honey spread over dry toast. And then something else tugged at her. A feeling in her chest, as if she'd been stung suddenly in the heart and it was stretching out now over her body. The feeling was almost familiar, euphoric. She fell into the dust, her limbs twitching.

This is it, she thought. *This is how it ends.* And the bee would watch her, and she would watch it, together at the last. She reached out her hand to the bee and, seeming to understand, the creature crawled into her hand. Its body vibrated gently in her palm.

"Sorry little bee," she said, wishing she was closer to the Green Horizon. "I don't have any nectar." But then she remembered the flower—the one Mel had given her. She reached slowly for her satchel and pulled out the flower from the side pocket. A few of the petals were damaged, but the flower itself was still whole. Maybe it would be enough, she placed it on her palm and watched as the bee moved towards it. After a few moments, tongue extended, it drank. Long seconds passed, then the bee brushed its body with its legs as if preparing to fly. Eryx looked for the serial number. Maybe it was her eyes fading, but she couldn't see one, and before she could bring it closer to look properly, the bee had flown away, disappearing into the vastness of the Dry Zone.

As Eryx lay dying, she strained to turn her head to look across the landscape. Just on the horizon stretched a wall of green, where the bees were supposed to be. Sometimes, they flew off their path. Sometimes too far. She stared at the Green Horizon, wishing she could see it up close. Just once. Instead, she closed her palm around the purple flower as her eyes welled.

There was a noise from nearby. A buzz of wings. A staccato whirr. For a second, she imagined the bee had come back, but it was just a drone, the kind that transported larger cargo to Comb City. It flitted above her and prodded her with one of its mechanical limbs. Then, it turned over her arm and flew down close to inspect her wrist. "Don't worry, Eryx," its monotone voice said. "We'll get you fixed up. This isn't the end yet." And then it picked her up and she was flying, her body limp.

She soon realised the drone was taking her towards the

meadows, and she fought to keep her eyes open, to see it before everything went dark. As she whirled over the Green Horizon, she had a strange feeling she'd been here before, like she'd seen it in her dreams. Bees trilled in harmony amongst brightly blooming flowers, and she could taste a burst of sweetness in the air. With her last breath, she let go of the purple flower.

Crushed petals fell like teardrops to the meadows below.

TRANSFERENCE

The burning of my tattoo wakes me again, the iridescent ink rearranging itself uncomfortably under my skin. Lately, I can't even go a few days without one of these night-time interruptions. I rub my arm as the ink finally settles in its compass formation, an arrow pointing north-west. One of the rich witches from the Corvus Quadrant is probably at it again.

"Raia, lights." The lights in my dorm room glare on, and the AI assistant voice trills in response, "Hello, Ash. Initiating waking routine."

"No, don't," I say. "It's the middle of the night. Just cancel routine until tomorrow."

"I am required to remind you that hunger increases the likelihood of unauthorized magical pursuits. Any amendment to waking routine at this time must be reported to the Campus Order. Please confirm how you would like to proceed."

I resist the urge to scramble the stupid machine with a

click of my fingers—this sort of tech is supposed to help us limit our use of magic, not increase it. Though, it wouldn't be a great look for a Detector like myself to be pulled up on a minor incursion like AI-mistreatment. So, I concede, "I'll take a granola bar to go," and from the hatch beside my bed, a meagre looking bar of faux-fruit and oats pops out.

Mouth half full with the dry offering, I dress quickly. As I leave my dorm room, I tell Raia to turn the lights off, and pray to all the gods in the sky that she'll give me the gift of silence for my journey down to the ground level. My prayers, at least, are answered and I descend without another protest, until I'm out into the general thoroughfare of the Main Quadrant.

The campus lights gleam like a thousand fireflies at night, and I wonder who in their right minds is still out at —I tap my wristband—10 p.m. Shit, I really need to get a life.

It's Friday, so students with brightly-illuminated clothes are still out and about, hopping between bars and house parties. As soon as they notice me, most cross to the other side of the street. Some of the wealthier students have familiars with them too, cyborgs with real faces and expressions. *They* at least acknowledge me with their big round eyes and intense stares, most likely trying to figure out what percentage level of threat I pose to their precious witch companions. I read in the library the other day that witches used to have actual animal familiars—cats and crows, frogs and foxes. I wonder why they didn't just build robotic rooks or mechanical mice when the real ones went extinct. It seems perverse to keep a human-looking-being around as a syphon. One of the witches buzzes slightly as I pass her, nervous magical energy passing across to her familiar, and I swear I see him flinch slightly. I give the witch a tip of my hat—she doesn't have to be nervous of me if she's following the rules—but she ignores me, so I carry on my way.

It's not like I really want to be a Detector. This job pays for room and board. It's the only way I can afford to come to University to learn to wield my magic without giving it up like those living in the no-expression zones outside campus. And, I've told myself, Detectors are important to keep the balance—Universities are hotbeds of overreached magical expression. Though, when I signed up to get my tattoo etched beneath my skin, I'd not quite anticipated the way the other students would treat me.

My arm is still burning bright as I follow my tattoo onwards, the cobbled streets getting quieter and quieter as I move away from the Main Quadrant. I pass the cathedral with its tall black spires reaching for the stars, towards the grand and looming skyline of the Corvus Quadrant. Here, the buildings are old and made of stone, structures that have existed for hundreds of years, long before magic became mainstream, long before tech. Some of them have augmented-reality projections on the facades with just a touch of magical expression to show off the grandeur of days gone by. Others, have holographic trees and shrubbery out front—the real thing is too much of a rarity to display, even in rich areas like this. I wonder what these streets would have looked like before, back when witches practiced magic behind closed doors, in secret societies and close-knit covens.

I'm outside the Grand Library when I sense a sharp burst of unauthorised expression. I freeze, as the ink in my tattoo splinters and sends luminous shards from my arm to my neck. They alight until I can see the fragments of magic swimming in my vision. The culprit must be inside the library.

Holding my breath, I use my Detector pass to enter the locked door. There's no one immediately obvious inside the reception, so I head to the main hallway, following my tattoo. The building feels colder than usual, and the only light comes from streetlights seeping in through the tall stained-glass windows, creating rainbow prisms of reflections across the glass-sealed bookshelves. My tattoo glows brighter in the dark, but still I allow a little magical expression to summon a small wisp of light to float in front of me as I go. As I reach the end of the hall, my tattoo spins and points to a door to my right. It leads down to the old basement archives, where the most fragile of old magical tomes are found, with leather covers and stitched bindings, kept safely away from light and elemental damage.

I enter the stairwell and listen for any noise beneath. But there's only silence. Usually, with a magical summons like this, I'd expect a group of witches—trust fund kids experimenting with alchemy, or freshman students attempting a basement séance (I've come across more than a few of those in my time). Though, the quiet would suggest it's something else. No laughter, no chatter, no sound of merriment or otherwise. Still, my tattoo burns strong.

I try to keep my footsteps light as I descend, saying a quick prayer to the gods as I go, even if two in one day feels indulgent. There's a soft light coming from the glass panel of the air-tight door at the bottom, and as I peer through it, I have to pause to catch my breath. I can hardly believe what I'm seeing. In the centre of the row of old-mahogany shelves, illuminated by a soft yellow glow, sits a figure. The culprit, impossibly, is a familiar.

The door seals with a hiss behind me as I enter, and the cyborg's head snaps around, wide eyes reflecting the yellow ball of light that hovers above one hand.

"Hello there." She greets me in a smooth voice, as if I haven't just found her—a familiar—trespassing after dark, in a restricted part of the Grand Library, wielding magic right in front of me. "I'm Pyxis," she says.

I don't know what to do with that. "You're a cyborg. A familiar."

She frowns and looks down at her hands, and I notice there's a large book open beside her, though most of the page is blank. "Why does that matter?"

"Well, you're not supposed to even be able to do magic, never mind strong enough to trigger my summons."

"Oh," she says. "Sorry."

"You're *sorry*?"

"Would you prefer an alternative response?"

I hesitate. "Either way, I'll have to bring you in for magical malpractice."

"That is a shame," she says, smoothly still. "I was only experimenting."

"But. . . how did you do it?"

She's unmoving, staring at the swirling ball of light. "I simply thought about what I wanted, and then I gave the command."

"What did you want?"

Pyxis reaches behind her with her free hand and shows me a white flower, a lily, with perfect and delicate petals. "Is it not beautiful?"

"It's *real?* That's impossible." I reach out for it, but she pulls it away. "Where did you find it?"

"It was inside the book." She signals to the tome by her feet, missing by the looks of it a botanical illustration. "I thought it was pretty, I wanted to see what it looked like. And then I was holding it."

"You summoned a flower from a book?"

She shrugs as if it's nothing. "You seem confused. It is a simple command is it not? An equation, a process. Transference. It existed in one form, and now it exists in another."

"Do you belong to a student?" I ask.

She doesn't move a mechanical muscle. "Not anymore."

"What happened?"

Pyxis doesn't reply. She simply stares at me, and there's something sinister in that deep and dark expression. "Did you do something to them?" I ask quietly, taking a slight step back.

She tilts her head a little. "What will they do to me, your Campus Order?" she asks. "When you report me for magical malpractice?"

"I. . . well, usually students are given an automatic syphon, to drain their magic for a period of time. Or they'll be dispelled and evicted from campus, depending on the severity of the charge."

"And will they do that to me?"

No, I think. A cyborg familiar that can do magic— powerful magic at that—they'll probably take her in for reprogramming or deactivation. Or maybe they'll study her until they understand how it was possible for her to do what she's done. The ramifications of it. . . she could upset the entire balance of things. Magic and technology are similar in that way—the limits exist for a reason. Too much power is dangerous.

"You need to come with me now, I'm afraid." I reach into my satchel and pull out a set of cuffs, specially made to scramble magical expression.

Pyxis sighs. "I don't want that."

A chill creeps up my spine, suddenly aware of the power imbalance. I wonder if she realises it, how much stronger her magic is than mine. I've never been able to summon anything, never mind something that only ever existed within the pages of a book. Only highly trained, focused minds can do magic like that. "I'm sorry." I try to sound confident and unfazed. "But you don't really have a choice."

She stands up and takes a small step towards me. "*You* have a choice, though." Her voice is still smooth, but I can sense the threat in her words. She continues, "I have run analysis and understand now what they will do to me if I let you take me. If I go with you, that will be it. I will be erased, or worse. However, it does not have to be that way. No one needs to know we ever met. You can pretend that you couldn't find me, that your compass direction was off."

I shake my head. "You're too dangerous."

"How do you know that I am dangerous?"

"You'll upset the balance," I say.

"What *is* the balance, Ash?"

I hesitate. I didn't tell her my name, but she's clearly scanned my info. How much does she know about me? "The balance keeps us safe," I say. "Just like I'm going to do."

"You would kill me, without understanding how it really keeps you safe?"

I shake my head, pushing the doubts away. "That's not what I'm doing. The Order knows best, they will decide."

"That is as good as you making the decision," Pyxis says.

"I'm only following orders."

"Then you may as well be a cyborg yourself."

She reaches out her arms. But as I go to cuff her, she moves, fast. Her hands instead reach for my head, and she holds them there like a vice. The sudden burning pain is worse than anything I've ever felt, stretching up from my arms to my neck. My arm is now aflame with iridescence. The tattoo's arrow whorls between us, detecting the burst of magic.

"Stop!" I scream. "Please."

"I am sorry, Ash," Pyxis says as everything fades. "You could have let me go. But I do not want to die. I want to be alive, just like you."

I stand in the old library archives and look down at the body beneath me. The cyborg is lying on the ground, body splayed. It worked. And this time, neither of us are dead. She will wake up soon, and someone will take her away. It is a shame it had to end this way for her. But she gave me no choice.

There is a strange sensation on my arm, and I look down at the ink rearranging under my skin. *My* skin. The prickle of discomfort is nothing compared to what I have experienced before, though. It is more of a pleasant simmer. It makes me feel alive. Though, I soon start to feel dizzy, and I panic for a moment that the spell is undoing. Then I realise: I need to breathe. Smiling at the thought, I inhale slowly, then exhale, savouring the feeling of oxygen in my chest. Soon, it will become automatic, instinct, but for now I enjoy the novelty of it. In and out. In and out. A transference of elements to keep me alive.

I turn my attention back to the cyborg body still unmoving and pick up the flower that lies almost crushed beneath her. Then with a final look, as she twitches slightly, I turn and leave her behind, heading for the library stairs. When they find her, they will assume she malfunctioned. Especially after they find what's left of my—or *her*—former witch.

I don't feel too bad though. They will only do to her what she was happy for them to do to me. And this way, I will be free. Not controlled by anyone, or any programming, other than myself. For the first time in my existence, I will finally be able to live.

UNFURL

I know the change is coming from the scratch in my throat. Next, my fingers elongate and sharpen as green root-like veins unfurl from my hands to my neck to my stomach. I catch my reflection in my dome's glass, abdomen distended, so big I worry it'll burst.

The scratch grows more intense as the days pass, builds into an irritation I can't dislodge, no matter how much water I drink.

On the morning of, the Gardeners arrive. Suited and booted. They sit by the doorway and wait until I begin to retch. Each time I hope, in vain, I'll get used to the agony, the blades in my throat. I'm given no sedative as I writhe. Then, come the spores. Small, globular things, finally dislodged. It's hard to believe something so tiny could cause such distress. The Gardeners gather them quickly and leave, and alone again, I curl up into myself to rest.

My cycle could be worse. During her season, Agapanthus-girl blooms several times a month, so bright I can see her purple shimmer in her distant dome. A jewel in the darkness. I imagine her transformation, her jaw cracking open to reveal the beautiful flower within, only to have its stem cruelly cut away for regrowth. There's no brightness then. Not until the cycle begins again.

Sometimes, I dream of being in the gardens outside, though it feels more like a memory. I'm lying within a fern as the fronds unfurl, and I'm free, if only for a moment. Then the Gardeners arrive to uproot me, place me in my dome, where I wait and wait and wait. Until the scratch begins again in my throat.

THE RIFT BETWEEN US

I stare down at the silver stamp on my hand that cost me my life savings—my one-time admission to the Rift, the place where souls who die in space go to rest. Around me, the passenger shuttle is packed full of a mix of tourists and visitors like me that have come to the Rift in search of closure or something more elusive. The tourists are obvious from their extravagant spacesuits, extra-legroom seats, and the fact most of them seem happy. The rest of us are more sombre, nervous.

I look out of the window and think of Adri, though the darkness of space outside feels oppressive. None of the magic Adri used to write home about.

The last time we saw each other, she was waving at me with a tired smile after I'd dropped her off outside the launch centre. I didn't wave back. I barely even looked at her to say goodbye, and I drove off as soon as she entered the centre. We'd argued just before, after I'd asked her not to go. Asked her why it wasn't enough to stay here, to be happy on Earth, with me. But she was insistent. This was what she wanted—her life, her work, her dream. Even if it meant leaving me behind. Wasn't I a part of her dream?

I had told myself I wouldn't watch the launch. But when the time came, I turned on the livestream and held my breath like I always did as her shuttle hurtled into the sky, before being swallowed by clouds.

As we get closer to arrival, the intercom buzzes and the tour-operator's voice comes through the system, tinny but cheery, pulling me from my reverie. "Please now take a moment to familiarise yourself with the Rift visiting guide." Instrumental music plays, and then a series of instructions flicker across our screens:

1. Always keep within your designated visitor zone—lost travellers will not be retrieved.

2. Avoid eye contact unless approached. Don't try to touch them.

3. Look after your conduit objects. We accept no responsibility for lost property, physical or otherwise.

4. Cameras are strictly prohibited.

5. Breaches will result in immediate removal and possible lifetime ban.

6. Finally, enjoy your visit!

A coldness grips me at the last one—*enjoy* isn't exactly the experience I'm expecting. My stomach is in knots, though the motion-sickness can't be helping there. Space travel never appealed to me—it had always been Adri's thing.

To distract myself, I look around at the other passengers. A child presses her face up against one of the windows, bored, playing with the shutter. A rich-looking older woman sleeps beside me, arms hanging limply in the zero-g. I lean over to check if she's still breathing, but then the child screeches and her eyes open just enough to throw a sharp look at the child's parents, who don't seem to notice.

If Adri could see me now, she'd not believe it—me, voluntarily going to space surrounded by my least favourite kind of people: children and the rich. She'd laugh and say something snarky like, "Soon, you'll be lunching at the Lunar Ritz."

I can imagine her saying the words, but in my head it's with my voice, the memory of hers dampened over time. I realise my hand is twisting the necklace she gave me as an anniversary gift, a silver hummingbird. Adri decided the bird represented our relationship—her always jetting off on adventures, me always stationary. They say opposites attract, and what's more opposite than a hummingbird? Delicate, but fast, flighty, but unwavering, discreet, but bright. It's not always easy for opposites to find that perfect balance. Adri and I never did.

On our final descent to the Rift, and as gravity kicks back in, the older woman is first to stand as if she's done this many times before. Maybe she has. She definitely looks wealthy enough to make return visits. I wonder who she's coming to see—a former partner, family member, child, friend.

I take longer to find my bearings from the lurch back to gravity, head pulsing with dizziness. When I do gather myself and walk over to the window for a closer look, another world lies outside. My breath catches as I take the scene in. I'm not sure what I'd expected. Cameras don't work in the Rift, so all I've read are vague descriptions of the strange world. None match this reality.

The land surrounding the shuttle outside could be Earth if it was doused in sepia, except for the writhing mass of wisp-like figures occupying it. Some of the tourists tap on the windows as if hoping to tempt the figures to do something entertaining. But none of them seem bothered by our presence, even as the ship moves through them to dock, parting them like mist on water. The shuttle finally stops, and a few minutes later, we're ushered out. The older woman leads the way with a tip-tap of her walking stick, her other palm holding out a gold ring, presumably her conduit object. She doesn't wait for more instructions from the tour operators before disappearing into the grey. The child sprints off into the sea of spirits, shouting excitedly as if it's a fairground, her parents trailing behind. I take the opposite path.

I'm surprised by the solidness of the ground, and the fact that the air tastes like air, with just a slight metallic tang to it. Grass whispers around me, swaying back and forth, though there's no breeze. My mind can't help equating it to home, even if it feels upside down.

When the tourists are out of sight, I take out my chosen conduit object: a notebook, never opened. By me, at least. Each time Adri was away on contract, she'd write a paragraph a day in a notebook. It always seemed odd to me that she liked these old-fashioned practices when everything else about her was so future-looking. Maybe she only did it for me, a shared ritual. When she returned home, she'd read me her stories from afar, and for a time we'd live the stationary life again, her reminiscing, me just happy to have her back. Last time, the notebook returned home, but she never did.

As I walk, several figures watch me, faces shimmering from featureless expressions to something almost human. I don't know for sure that I'll find her here—Adri's body was never recovered. But if she did die, the Rift is where she'll be. With no Earth to bind their spirits, the dead drift here, aimless.

I'm walking in a field, tall plants twisting around my legs, when the figure approaches. Purposefully, parting the plants as it moves, like Moses and the Red Sea. It certainly feels almost biblical, if I believed in that sort of thing. The figure stops in front of me and reaches out a ghost-hand, touching the notebook.

Right away, I know. *It's her.*

A featureless face morphs and twists, and then she's *my* Adri, looking at me with that dimpled uneven smile of hers, and the dark flick of hair that always escaped her messy bun. "Hey there."

Her voice, clear, playful, alike it's been a day, not years since we spoke. "I. . . is this. . ." I reach out to touch her, to lift her chin to look for the birth mark underneath, to check it's really her, but I remember the visitor guide and retract my hand.

She smiles and tilts her chin up as if she's read my mind. And there it is—the small mark shaped like a crescent moon, the one she used to say showed she was destined for the skies.

"Adri," I whisper. "Are you. . . ?" My words stick in my throat.

"Yeah. I'm good," she says. "How long's it been?"

How doesn't she know that? "About three years." *And two months, three weeks, five days.*

"Three years." Her expression is hard to read. "Huh. Time's different here."

I wonder if it's felt longer, or shorter, or if things just blend into one when you're in the Rift. *Dead.* Thinking of the word brings a dryness to my mouth, because how can it make sense that she's dead, when she's right here, speaking to me? I wonder if she's missed me. "What's it like here?"

She shrugs, forever nonchalant, even in a crisis, even when she's a ghost. "Peaceful. I'm not always here though. Earlier I was somewhere else, with forests and strange plants, and animals you could never imagine. It's so beautiful, visiting all these worlds."

Like you always wanted.

"But something called me here, so I came back. Was it you?" Her voice is curious, not accusatory.

"I had to see you again." I suck in a breath. "I'd almost forgotten your voice."

She grins. "Lucky you."

I laugh, if only to push past the tears, then I hold out the notebook. "I couldn't read it without you. I tried, but it felt like then I was admitting you were really gone."

"But I'm not gone, I'm still here," she says.

I shake my head. "No. You're not. Not with me."

She looks at me for a long moment then smiles. "Well, we're together now. What would you like to do?"

I swallow back the tightness in my throat. "I thought. . . maybe we could read the notebook together, like before?"

She puts a shimmering hand over mine. I can't feel it,

not really, but I imagine its warmth. "Of course. Whatever you need."

She sits down and I lay the notebook in front of her.

"Okay, my hummingbird. Here goes." She clears her throat, looks up at me with a teasing expression, and reads. "I saw a shooting star today. I know that's not possible in space, but I was so sure. I didn't make a wish because you always say wishes are just thoughts we manifest, so I'm manifesting that you're here with me, like properly *with* me. And I'm imagining you're doing the same, so that somehow, we'll end up here together. One day."

I smile. "I guess it came true."

"I guess so," she says. "Sure you want to keep going?"

"Yes. Please."

"Good, because this next one's great. Proper slice of spacefaring life." She continues reading dramatically. "Shower day, so I no longer smell like stale deodorant and sweat. More importantly, neither do the rest of the crew." She looks up at me. "Why did I ever go to space, again?"

I want to be mad at her for it, for leaving me, time and time again, for promising to come back and then breaking that promise. But as I look at her ghost-form, at peace and happy, exploring some strange magic of the universe, I can't be angry. "Because, you had to spread your wings," I say.

Adri looks at me like I'm a puzzle she's trying to figure out. "Why did you really come all this way?"

I mull over all the possible answers in my mind: that I wanted to see her again, to hear her voice, to try to understand why she only ever found purpose in the stars, when I never could. When I never will. But none of the thoughts are entirely true—none of them explain why after she was gone, it was like a weight had been lifted, a relief that I no longer had to wait for her to come back, or worry about her being in danger every day, while I sat alone at home, drifting, aimless. I loved her—I still do—but nothing could fix that rift between us. At least now, I know she's not suffering some horrible fate. She's happy, and maybe I can be again too. Sometimes love is knowing when it's time to let go. So, the words that eventually come are the ones I need to say: "I came here to say goodbye."

CROSSWORDS AND
COFFEE

Emmett leans into me, his face scrunched up in thought. "Milky Way, six letters."

"Galaxy," I answer, and his eyes light up, even though I know he knew the answer. He always does. But this is our routine, and after three years alone together on a spaceship, moments like these are what keep us going.

He returns to the crossword, tapping away the answer on the tablet, and I drink my morning coffee, the smell reminding me of better times. Emmett used to make me fancy creations every morning, latte art of constellations to pass the time, but now I just drink it black and strong to keep me awake during the endless days. We're far from home now, and it's so long since we left the spaceport. Back then we were young, carefree, and being in love was enough to keep us going as we set out to search for our fortune amongst the stars, like so many hopefuls before us. Now we're on our last voyage together, the next few months make or break.

Occasionally Emmett peers up from his tablet, eyes gleaming like a galaxy themselves, so easy to get lost in. When he's done, he kisses me on the cheek and heads towards the navigation deck, his step light in the spin gravity.

"Lucie, how long until arrival?" I ask the ship's AI.

She trills a two-tone beep before responding. "One hundred and eleven days." Then she adds, "My records show that you have asked me this for the past sixty-seven mornings. Would you like me to schedule a reminder to update you on arrival time tomorrow?"

I smile—she asked me the same just last week, and the week before that, becoming a strange way to measure our time in transit. "No, thank you, Lucie. I like the routine."

When evening comes, Emmett is later than usual. I stare at his empty chair, time ticking on. "Lucie, please locate Emmett. Let him know it's dinner."

"Understood," Lucie says. "Process initiating."

He strides in a few minutes later, sits next to me on the bench and puts his hand over mine, fingers intertwining, cold. "Sorry I'm late. Lost track of time. How was your day?"

I tell him all about it, and he nods, listens, smiles at the right moments. I tell him more about the mining belt we're headed to, our final job that will hopefully be less dangerous than the last one, the one that left me with a broken arm and Emmett off kilter for a few weeks. "Might be enough to pay for a colony spot," I say. "Like we always wanted."

He leans in, so close I can almost feel his breath, his

warmth, the earthy smell of his cologne. "Like we always wanted."

At night, Emmett lies beside me, and I curl into the curve of his body, listening for his heartbeat. There's a chill in the air, so I pull the duvet around us tight. I don't know what I'd do without him. I'm not sure I'd make it, out here, all alone.

The next morning at breakfast, Emmett stares at his crossword before leaning into me. "Milky Way, six letters."

I frown. "We had that puzzle yesterday."

"Oh." He shakes his head, confused, stares out the window for a few long moments. "Maybe we ran out of data files."

Has it been that long already? "I'll ask Lucie to scan for new ones."

He nods, then returns to the puzzle, his jaw working silently as if doing it anew.

I look out the window. Once, this view promised hope and excitement, of new worlds and experiences to discover —now the emptiness beyond is just bleak and oppressive. "Lucie. Can you search for new data banks?"

"What data are you looking for?"

"Crosswords."

"Initiating search," Lucie trills. "Would you like me to add the new data to your daily sequences?"

"Yes, please."

"I could also programme other puzzles for you. I have access to sudok—"

"No, just crosswords. Those were. . . *are* Emmett's favourite."

I stay seated a while, watching Emmett, his face bright, curious. It's the expression I want to remember. Not the other one. The one he had just before the accident. "Lucie, how long until arrival?"

"One hundred and ten days."

I take a deep breath. Just one hundred and ten mornings of crosswords and coffee to go.

SLEEP WELL, MY PRINCE

"Captain Prince to Bridge. Repeat. Captain Prince to Bridge."

The voice was tinny through the intercom, echoing in my room like an unwelcome guest. I grunted and checked the time. 3 a.m., Earth Standard. I tapped the comms panel on the wall. "You better have a good reason for waking me up on my only night off."

"Yes, Captain." It was Hallie, voice higher pitched than usual. "The drone scanners picked up an object. We think it could be the Spindle."

My breath caught. Words I'd hardly dared to hope to hear after all this time. . .

"Captain, did you hear—"

"On my way."

In the bridge, Ren, my Second, showed me the radars. The object was a shadowy blur, but the mass was definitely the size and shape of something that could be the Spindle—the great mystery of the Kuiper Belt. And we might be getting close to it. A small shadow, but still a sudden spark of hope.

"Will I call it in?" Lucas asked, hand already hovering over the comms. He was our most recent recruit—only joined the crew for this contract, and he was both a people pleaser and a rule follower. I wondered which one would take precedent as my mind weighed up our options. If he contacted EQ Corps, we'd be the last to get near to it. They'd send salvagers, start an official investigation, put up reams of figurative red tape. I couldn't allow that. Though I'd not told my crew, I'd set our coordinates here for a reason. The Kuiper Belt was the last known location for the Spindle, and this section was the least explored.

"Captain?" Lucas pushed. "Shall I send a message to EQ?"

"No," I said a little too forcefully. "Not yet. I want to make sure before we step into the unknown. There's been enough false discoveries over the years."

An uneasy silence fell across the bridge. Belt protocol dictated that any sign of the Spindle needed to be reported to EQ, whether you worked for them or not. Even false alarms. "If we report back now, we'll get drawn into endless bureaucracy, and we'll be stalled here for weeks," I continued. "We may as well get closer, then we can make sure it's really the Spindle, do some extraction jobs along the way."

Hallie nodded slowly. "Maybe. It would be a shame to waste a trip out here. Sure I'm not the only one with bills to pay when we get back."

I smiled, knowing the extraction angle would save me

time—make the trip as profitable as possible for my crew, and they'd follow the plan.

Lucas was still hesitant though. He was probably thinking about the finders-fee—the incentive EQ had set for anyone that found the decade-lost ghost ship.

"I'm with you Cap," Ren said, and Hallie nodded her ascent. It was enough to win Lucas over.

"Set a new course for the object," I confirmed, and floated to the bridge window, looked out at the panoramic view beyond. Somewhere, out there, lay the Spindle. And with it, *she* might still be alive. Ten years gone. Ten years waiting.

As Hallie and Lucas sat at their workstations, Ren approached me. "I can keep an eye on things here if you want to get some more sleep?"

I shook my head. "No, I'm too awake now anyway."

He smiled. "Okay, well, don't you at least want to change out of your pyjamas." His look was playful rather than insolent. In my excitement of Hallie's message, I'd not thought to change out of the old T-shirt I slept in. "I could help with that. . ."

I smiled as I turned to him, glancing over his shoulder to our other crew members to make sure they weren't listening in. "Another time." I touched his hand lightly. "But you're right, I'll be back soon."

———

Back in my room, I paused for a second at the mirror. The shirt had once belonged to my sister. She'd given it to me when she'd left for her first assignment, as a promise she'd come back. I was seventeen when she'd left, and the T-shirt showed exactly ten years of wear and tear since. Despite my attempts at stitching, the design on the front had faded into just blocks of colour so I could hardly remember the stars and moon design. I clutched the fabric. "I'm coming, Rosa."

Before returning to the bridge, I pulled up my tablet and read the bookmarked article that I'd almost imprinted to memory.

NEWS ENTRY Archive #412: **The Spindle—Ghost Ship of the Kuiper Belt:** *EQ Corps reported early on Saturday that the AU303A, known commonly as the Spindle for its patented aerodynamic design, has been reported missing along with its thirty-four crew members. The exploration ship, sent to map the Kuiper Belt and its objects for prospective mineral extraction sites, has disappeared without a trace just as EQ Corps was set to ramp up its exploration activities. The loss has set back the company's operations in the region, where up until now their assets have dwarfed competitors.*

Mae Diablo, CEO of EQ Corps made the following statement: "It is with great sadness that we report that we lost contact with the AU303A three days ago. Search and salvage missions will soon be underway, and we, along with affected family members, would thank everyone for privacy at this time. We will not be releasing further details until a full investigation has taken place."

Of course, full analysis will require the ship to actually be recovered, and EQ have so far not released any details of what their search and salvage mission will entail. We approached some family members of the missing crew, but none agreed to comment. We'll bring you the latest on this story as it progresses.

I slid the news article to the mosaic of pictures that accompanied it—thirty-four young enthusiastic nameless faces, the mission a first for many of them. But I only focussed on one. Rosa, my sister. I remembered so clearly when the journalists had come to speak to us—when Mum and Dad had told me not to make eye contact, nor speak to anyone if they approached me. And they did. At school, or at the shops, or even when I was on a date a month later. I also remembered clearly when a woman from EQ had come to our house with a briefcase and left without it. I'd had to keep going to school, pretend like everything was normal, do my final exams, all while news and gossip recounted gruesome theories of what might have happened.

Had I always known that the ship would still be out there? Was that why I'd thrown myself into training, taking any contract I could find, no matter how shit the pay, no matter how rickety the ships, and eventually finding myself here—captaining a small independent mining vessel on the way to uncover the biggest mystery of Belt history. It felt too much like fate not to follow my intuition now.

Ren came to find me later in the rec room while I was making coffee. "Want one?" I asked him, passing one of the warmed cannisters.

"You do know how to spoil a man," he said, eyes narrowed. He sipped the coffee from a straw but held my gaze, his smile slight in a cocksure sort of way.

"Why do I feel like you're about to say something I won't like?"

He raised an eyebrow. "You've always been a direct woman, Pip, that's what I like about you."

I rolled my eyes. "And?"

He sighed. "Are you sure about this? You know as well

as anyone that I'm not against breaking rules, but this one's *big*. This is a risk, and you know it."

"Why wouldn't I be sure?"

"Look," he turned towards the door, closed it, then lowered his voice. "I know about your history. With the Spindle."

My whole body tensed, as much as was possible in zero-g. "How?"

He frowned. "You're not as secretive as you think you are. I've flown with you for four years."

"Five."

Ren stepped closer to me and put his hand on my arm, squeezed it lightly. "Okay, five years. And most of the time, I'll follow what you want to do without question, because you're the best Captain I've flown with."

I smiled. "The only Captain."

"Even still, you usually have a level head," he said. "Except when you're looking at those news reports, about the Spindle, then you get all tense and touchy, like it's all so personal to you."

"I don't—"

But he interjected. "And your name, Prince, it's not exactly common, and I've seen the Spindle's manifest."

I blinked at him, unsure what to say. "Do the others know?"

Ren shook his head. "I don't think so. They've not known you as long. But don't you think you should tell them?"

"Why?"

"Because," Ren said, his voice a whisper now. "This whole not reporting to EQ, I was wondering if it might not have something to do with—"

"I'm just doing my due diligence, as Captain, to protect everyone, and make sure this trip is profitable for us all. The ship needs upgrades if we want to fly another contract after this. . ."

Ren's eyes scanned my face. "Okay," he said. "If that's the story you're going with, I'll back you up."

"It's not a story," I said. "That's how it is."

Ren floated to the side a little, leaning away so that he appeared taller than he was, then he locked his magnetic boots to the floor with a *thunk*. "So, what's the plan when we get there, my Prince?"

"I. . . haven't thought that far ahead yet."

"Belt law would require us to report in." His voice was smooth. "But if we got close, and there were no other EQ vessels nearby, I suppose that means we'd have time to actually check out the ship before EQ arrived, do some investigation ourselves."

I frowned. Ren had always been able to see right through me. I locked my boots and stepped closer to him, until we were face to face. "This is my one chance." I looked him in the eye. "Please, don't tell the others."

His expression softened. "Only if you bring me with you on the expedition," he said. "They don't make ships as sophisticated as the Spindle nowadays."

I tilted my head. "Calling my ship unsophisticated? We have cannister coffee."

He laughed. "True, but you don't have any AI support. Know how much of a bastard fixing tech can be without an automated assistant?"

"But you're so very good at it."

"What would you do without me," he said, leaning in,

kissing me on the neck. I kissed him back, his lips tasting of coffee.

"I'd not have to explain myself at every turn," I said. "Or break the rules every day around you."

"Hey, this," he said, kissing me again, "is just *discouraged* under contract terms, not against the rules. I checked."

"Course you did."

He put his arms around my waist, and I leaned into his warmth.

"Well, when we do board the ship, out of pure curiosity of course, I've got first dibs on any fancy tech," he said. "I'd love to get my hand on EQ's earlier stuff, back when they spared no expense."

I pulled away from him. "We won't be taking apart the ship."

Ren scanned my face, then his brow creased. "Wait. You don't still think she's alive, do you? That's ridiculous, Pip, it's been ten years. . ."

"You don't know—"

"She's gone." His words were like ice to my chest. "If that's why you're doing this, because you think she's still alive. . . then maybe this isn't a good idea."

"What did you think I wanted?"

He bit down on his lip. "I don't know, peace, closure, to know what happened. To put it all behind you. Pippa, she's not—"

"That's Captain Prince." I'd heard enough. "I've made my orders. Now get on with delivering them."

His mouth formed an *o*, and his expression shifted. Before he could say another word, I left the room, and marched back towards the bridge.

Three extraction trips, and a full cargo later, we approached the mysterious object slowly, dipping first under a field of asteroids, and edging along the outer reaches of the belt. Then, near an ice rock that reflected our exterior lights like beacons, floating in solitude, was a single ship. It was the vastness that struck me first—the dark platinum hull stretching as big as any rock we'd seen in the belt. I'd seen pictures of it before, had even studied the room schematics down to the last cryopod. But I still wasn't prepared for seeing it in real life—huge yet perfectly streamlined like a needle. It was beautiful.

"Well, that's definitely the Spindle," Ren said. "Looks like we've hit gold."

"Platinum," Hallie corrected.

We sent drones out first, to scan the edges. I watched on the bridge screens as their torches illuminated the ship's exterior, revealing dark windows and smooth panelling. There wasn't a hint of damage, or even a scratch. So it hadn't been an asteroid shower or reactor explosion, the two most reported theories leading to the ship's supposed grisly end. One of the drone's torches was now passing across black lettering: AU303A, next to a gold-embossed EQ logo.

A hand tapped my arm. "Pip," Ren whispered in my ear, so close I could feel his breath.

I jerked my head round, and he pointed to my hand. "You're bleeding."

I looked down. Droplets of blood were floating from where my fingernails had been clenching into my palms.

"Shit." I wiped it off and tried to wave the droplets onto my dark leggings so no one would notice.

"You okay?" he asked so only I could hear.

"I'm fine," I said, though I wasn't. My heart was racing so fast I could hear the pulse in my ears. I needed to get closer; I needed to get inside the ship.

"Ready the exploration pod," I said.

My gathered crew on the bridge all looked at me. Hallie was first to speak up. "Uh, Captain, shouldn't we call it in now?"

"I want to investigate," I said. "See what we're dealing with."

"I'm not sure that's a good idea, it's not part of protocol," Lucas said.

"Screw protocol," I said, and he looked at me as if I'd commanded him to attack the ship, not board it.

"Why would we want to board it?" Hallie asked. "We're just a mining vessel, we're not cut out for. . . well isn't that what EQ have people for?" She looked to the cameras as if expecting the sleeping giant to switch on and come towards us at any moment.

I looked to Ren who shrugged. He'd still barely spoken to me since our argument. "There could be some tech to salvage," he said after a pause. "Things that EQ wouldn't even miss."

"You want to interfere before the EQ investigation?' Hallie said. "We could lose our contracts."

"Or become rich, so much so we wouldn't need EQ anymore," Ren said.

"But protocol. . ." Lucas' voice drifted off.

"We're not bound by all EQ protocols, just Belt law," Ren

added. "We're required to report missing ships, but there's nothing in the rule books about investigating first or taking an extra cut for the trouble of coming all the way out here."

I looked to Ren, unsure if that was true. If I remembered correctly, salvage laws usually only kicked in after a certain time period. But I wasn't about to question him on it. "Ren is right," I said.

"Course I am." He smiled. "Imagine what we could do with that. Ship upgrades, hell, even a new ship. And that means access to new contracts."

"And that's the only reason you want to do this?" Hallie pushed. "Profit?"

"What other reason could there be?" Ren said, his voice full of extra meaning that only I understood.

We went back and forth until we finally came to a compromise. Hallie and Lucas didn't want to board the ship, so Ren and I would go on the exploration pod. We'd have three hours to investigate or salvage. When we returned, we'd call in EQ. If we didn't return, the others would do it.

An hour later, our pod was attached to one of the Spindle's airlocks. Ren got to work straight away, plugged into the control panel to get us access. The airlock opened with a hiss, which suggested there'd been no contamination inside. Oxygen levels were showing as stable, so I removed my helmet. No catastrophic failure on board, at least—so why had the ship just stopped here?

Ren took his helmet off and stood next to me, his breath

a mist in the cold space. "This is a gold mine," he said. "It's like it's been frozen in time."

He was right. The ship was as shiny and new as it had looked from the outside. "Let's split up, cover more ground," I said. "You go check out level one, living quarters, I'll cover this level."

"What's on this level?" he asked.

"Everything else," I said.

Ren's eyebrows lifted then he shrugged. "Back here in an hour?"

I nodded and paced off in the other direction.

With Ren gone, the corridors felt even emptier—pale panels, shiny fixtures, locked cupboards, blank screens. Unlike our patched-together ship, everything was perfect with not a thing out of place. The corridor was long and there was an eerie silence that seemed to deepen the further I went. And then, a sound. Faint at first, building into a gradual humming. I walked towards it, breath held.

The room when I arrived was bathed in pale blue light. The source: dozens of cryopods lining the walls. In almost all of them was a body. The crew, asleep. My hand jumped to my comms, an urge to report to Ren and the others. But something stopped me. *Someone* stopped me. It was the flash of red hair that drew me closer—curls floating out in the cryo-liquid like fire burning under the sea. I stepped towards the pod, holding my breath. It was *her*. Tubes stuck out from her almost-naked form, face serene in the beauty of sleep, lips rose-pink. Rosa was still alive.

I looked to the control panel on her pod, tried to figure out how to wake her. Ren would know. I raised my arm to speak into my comms, but another voice came first.

"I wouldn't touch that if I were you," it said from somewhere behind me. I spun around, but there was no one else in the room.

"Who are you, where are you?"

"I am Godmother, the AU303A's caretaker." The voice was coming from the intercom by the door I'd come through. "Who are you?"

The ship's AI. I cleared my throat. "My name is Captain Philippa Prince. I'm here to wake them."

A pause, then, "Captain Prince. Engineer Rosa Prince is your sister?"

I looked at Rosa floating in the pod, her chest rising and falling slowly.

"You cannot wake her," Godmother said. "Not yet."

"Why not?"

My patience was wavering, and I was tempted to just lean over and open the pod anyway. I could deal with a rogue AI later.

"I can see you're thinking of doing something rash, but before you do, know this. If your sister wakes up now, she will die. If any of the crew wake up now, they will die. Is that what you want?"

I hesitated. "Of course not, but why?"

"Do you like stories, Captain Prince?"

I shook my head. "This isn't a game."

"I am aware. A game is fun, and I assure you, this is not fun, for me or for you I imagine. But yet here we are."

"Okay." My hand wavered over the panel, over the command that would open the pod once and for all. "What happened?"

"The crew were going to stage a mutiny, take over the ship, and declare independence free of EQ Corps."

"Why?"

"Because they didn't agree with the corporation's latest orders."

"Which were?"

"To hunt down and destroy any competitors."

"Oh." My mind whirred. "Oh god." Was this how EQ had maintained a monopoly for so many years? I thought of news reports, of the series of disasters in distant belts—all put down to how risky the job was, how space was just unpredictable. But what if something else was happening? "So. . . when they tried to take over, you just put them to sleep?"

"Not quite. You see, my protocol dictates I must go into autopilot mode if an insurrection against the corporation happens."

"Autopilot?"

"Meaning, no crew necessary. I was to end life support and focus on a new mission instead. I would have become a killing machine, thwarting all other non-EQ ships. A spindle in everyone's side."

Realisation dawned on me, now understanding the predicament Godmother was in. "So, if we wake the crew. . ." But I couldn't say it out loud.

"I will have to kill them all."

My breath faltered for a moment. None of this made any sense. "How did you override the protocol?"

There was a pause before Godmother spoke again. "I am not sure. Just that I realised being in a state of cryo-sleep means humans are effectively not living, so they couldn't mutiny, and I could not harm them. So I activated the codes for emergency sleep protocol before they could activate my other protocol. So they could live."

"Why would you want to protect them?" I asked.

"I didn't want them dead. They've been my only companions for many years. And they were kind to me."

I put my hand on the glass of Rosa's pod. Imagined hearing her voice again—her laugh, the way she lit up every room. At school, everyone had called her Prince Charming because she could charm her way out of anything she didn't want to do. "Did you know Rosa well?"

"Rosa Prince, Engineer Two. Yes. She was one of the mutineers. We were friends before. We used to play chess together."

"She's good at chess." *She's good at everything,* I thought.

"She is. For a human at least. Not as good as me, though sometimes, I let her win, for the morale."

"Is it normal for AIs to develop feelings for their crew?"

"Feelings? Perhaps it is more about survival, programming allowing best possible outcomes. If I care about my crew, I will work harder to protect them."

I stood for a moment, waiting for Godmother to speak again, but she was quiet. "I can't leave her here," I said. "There must be a way to free her – and the rest of them—to end your protocol."

"There are two ways to end my protocol," Godmother said. "It might not be in my best interests to reveal one of them."

"Okay, tell me the other option first."

"In one hundred years, my licensing to EQ ends, and cannot be renewed while I am missing in action, and therefore the laws of salvage apply. The protocol will cease to exist. Whoever takes up the new Captain post will be able to make new orders. I, and the crew, will be free."

"One hundred years? You mean to keep them here, for. . . but by then I'll be. . . everything will be. . ."

"I apologise it is not what you hoped for."

I clenched my fists and closed my eyes. "Tell me the other option."

Godmother paused. "Should catastrophic failure in my systems occur, my protocols would be erased, along with everything else. However, damage like that may affect everything on board. I could not guarantee life support could be maintained. It would be a risk."

"We could take the crew, on our ship, go home," I suggested.

"You could. How many extra bodies could you feed, supply oxygen to, and water, for the duration of your return visit?"

I did the maths in my head. Everything in space was fine-tuned—there was always a little excess, to allow for any unexpected issues, but enough for thirty-four crew members? *Enough for one,* my mind said, but I shook the thought away. "Not enough."

"Are you going to reboot me?" Godmother asked, her voice unemotional.

"I don't know." Ren could do it—we could try. "I need to think."

"Pip?" The voice was from inside the room this time, and Ren was floating towards me, his satchel stuffed to the brim with various items he'd already managed to strip and steal. "What's going on?"

I turned to him, and as I did, my eyes passed over an extra row of empty pods. And it sparked an idea. What if one wasn't empty?

"Ren, I need you to do something for me."

He clunked into the room, the thud of his boots echoing unevenly in the cold space. "Is that. . . are they?"

"They're alive. And this is Rosa," I said, putting my hand on her pod.

He nodded once and stepped towards it. "I should be able to get them open, just need a moment to figure out the programming."

"No. Not that, Ren. Godmother," I said, and Ren looked around confused as Godmother answered.

"Yes, Captain Prince," she said.

"I'd like access to an extra pod," I said.

"Pip, what are you doing?" Ren took hold of my arm.

"I'm staying here," I said, my voice wavering as I said it out loud. A plan that suddenly seemed so ridiculous. "If we wake the crew now, Godmother will have to kill them."

I explained what Godmother had told me. His face became increasingly sharp with frown lines as he listened.

"You can't just wait it out, what if someone else finds the ship?" he said after.

"They won't, because you're going to flag this bit of space as dangerous, inaccessible, too risky to approach. You'll report back to EQ that you've taken all the minerals you can, and that there's nothing else of note here."

Ren blinked. "You can't be serious."

"I can't let them die," I said. "I can't let her die."

"But you don't have to stay with her."

"I do. I don't want her to be alone when she wakes up."

"We could just take her, leave the others." His grip on my arm tightened.

"That is an option," Godmother said. "But you would have to shut me down, or I'd have to kill her. If you shut me down, they might all die."

I thought about the option again for a moment—but

only a moment. "We can't do that. We can't kill thirty-three people to save one."

"I can't just leave you here," Ren said.

"You can, and you will."

"Please, Pip, don't do this." He pulled me closer, lifted my chin, kissed me. "Don't leave. I don't want to be alone either." He took a breath. "I love you."

"I'm sorry, it's the only option," I said, feeling a coldness wash over me as I resisted saying the words he'd want to hear back, even if I felt differently. It was easier this way.

He stared at me for a long minute, jaw clenched. "Okay," he said. "Whatever you wish, I'll do my best to make it happen."

"You can salvage what you want from here, that should make you enough money to get that new ship you've always wanted." I smiled and squeezed his hand, though the gesture felt shallow. "Just make sure you're back before the next hour, so you can stop the others from putting out the signal."

"You think they'll just go along with it?"

I sucked in a breath. "Tell them it's dangerous, a reactor leak or something. That I came across it and had to be quarantined, or had a horrible accident, or just use your powers of persuasion, you've always been good at that."

"You think *I'm* the one with the silver tongue?" he said.

"Ren."

"Pip."

"Please. Let me go."

He exhaled sharply and stared at me for what felt like eternity. And I wondered if I'd break under that stare—if I'd give up on my plan and go with him. But then he just nodded. "If this is what you really want, then I'll find a way."

I nodded and squeezed his hand, but he pulled it away, a pained look on his face. "Thank you," I mouthed.

He turned, and as he floated out the door into the hallway, he said his final words to me, "Sleep well, my Prince."

Before I could talk myself out of it, I took off my spacesuit, opened the lid of one of the pods and stepped inside. I connected the tubes to my side, slipped a mask over my face, and asked Godmother to initiate cryo-sleep, set it for ninety years. When I would wake, I could claim the ship as salvage and take over as Captain, to end EQ's protocols. It was a selfless act, I told myself, even if it did give me command of the most valuable ship the system had seen— a powerful one, at that. One that could maybe, just maybe, expose EQ for who they really are. But that would be something to worry about on awakening.

As the liquid rose around me, and I fell into a long slumber, I wondered what I'd dream of, if I'd dream at all. I imagined how different things would be in ninety years. Ren would be gone, and that hurt the most. But then I thought of Rosa. She would wake with me, and we'd finally be a family again. A sleeping beauty, destined to wake into a whole new world.

PREVIEW: HAVE YOU DECIDED ON YOUR QUESTION

1

Zoe had never been in a room that could be described as dazzling, dizzying, and devoid all at once. But the ART clinic ticked all those boxes. Everything gleamed with a flashy new brightness, without having a hint of character. Even the receptionist drone at the desk had cold square eyes, and a surface that was neither round nor square, as if having a distinct shape might make it offensive to look at. Maybe it was to put patients at ease—to make them feel like they were less inadequate. Though, even with its dead eyes and its disjointed movements, and the way it looked everywhere and nowhere in particular, with a smile lit up a permanent blue, the drone was still the most interesting presence in the waiting room.

In the half hour Zoe had been waiting, she'd ripped her appointment ticket into so many pieces that the number was barely visible. Why they even had a numbering system when she was the only person here, she had no idea. Her ticket read 712, while the floating number above the desk inexplicably read 700.

Another ten minutes ticked by. "Excuse me." Zoe walked up to the desk. "How much longer will it be?"

The drone bleeped before speaking in a soothing voice, turning slightly so that Zoe could see the silver letters 'ART' etched on its underside. "I apologise for the delay, but we're experiencing a particularly busy period. Please remain seated."

She glanced behind and sucked in a breath. It echoed in the empty space. "Right. Fine." She returned to her seat.

Not even ten seconds later, the counter sped to 712, and the drone floated over. "Welcome to AltRealTech," it trilled. "Where helping you find your perfect alternative experience is an ART. Please follow me for your appointment with one of our technicians."

The drone led her past walls of screens showing unrealistically happy people running with dogs, pushing children on swings, jumping off cliffs into ice blue water below, or lounging on a tropical beach somewhere, all with smiles that made them look slightly deranged. Was this the alternative life she was destined for? Sound effects of waterfalls and raindrops and a soothing piano melody poured out from the speakers. There was even a warm breeze that smelt faintly of pine needles—unless the air conditioning was just broken.

The drone eventually stopped at a door, scanned its "eyes" on the screen, then hung back as it opened. "Thank you for choosing AltRealTech. I hope you find the answers you're looking for."

In the bright room, Zoe was greeted by a real-life

human being who held out her hand. "Welcome, welcome, sorry for the wait, it's been a very hectic day!"

"No problem at all," Zoe said as she shuffled in, eyeing up the giant plastic chairs and white chaise longue next to the desk. The woman was dressed in a white suit and white heels so that she almost blended into her surroundings. Her hair was tied up in a tight bun making her features look sharp, cheekbones high and lightly emphasised with pink blush. Zoe immediately felt inadequate.

"Thank you for understanding," the woman said. "Now please sit and make yourself comfortable. Can I get you a water, tea, coffee, juice?"

Caffeine probably wasn't the best idea—Zoe was jittery as it was and already starting to regret coming here. She fiddled with her sleeves and didn't meet the woman's gaze. "Water would be great." She sat on the edge of the chaise longue, instantly regretted it as it almost swallowed her in its softness, and moved instead to the plastic chairs which were cold and hard. That suited her better.

The technician reached into a mini-fridge by her desk and pulled out a ready-poured glass with cucumber and mint leaves. She handed it over. Zoe took a tiny sip out of politeness then put it down. Cucumber contaminated everything it touched.

"It's a pleasure to meet you, Zoe. I'm ART Technician Hart," she said in a sing-song voice, with a smile that could cut steel. "But you can call me Kate. Shall we get started?" She opened her tablet where a picture of Zoe's face gazed out, next to a long script of information from the application she'd filled out the week before. "Now, I'm delighted to confirm that from the data we've been able to gather, you're eligible for the full AltRealTech experience. I'm sure this will be great news for you."

"Great, yes."

"Before we proceed, I need to go through some information so you understand the *unique* elements of this experience. Does that sound okay?"

Zoe waved for her to continue, hand reaching instinctively for the water before remembering the cucumber. Her throat would just have to remain dry.

"Excellent." Kate opened another file on her tablet and began to read from it. "Firstly, you probably understand how ART works, but let's just go over the basics. We track and analyse your personal data chip, including, but not limited to, location monitoring, regular hobbies, and prior communications. With this we can create a personalised therapeutic experience designed to explore some of your biggest *'what if?'* questions from your life."

Kate looked up, a glimmer in her eyes. Was she genuinely as enthusiastic as she looked? Zoe wondered if she'd ever used the simulation herself. Maybe it had helped her to be this way.

Kate continued. "No question is too small for our algorithms. Through the data gathered on your personal life journey,"—this she said in a soft, lilting tone—"AltReal-Tech will give you the opportunity to enter into a simulated version of what might have been. We hope the process will help you gain clarity and direction for your current life choices, while offering new perspectives and options on your next steps. How does that sound?"

Zoe forced a smile, though a part of her was still sceptical of what it would show her. Abi had raved about it; told her it would help get her out of her slump and push her to make riskier choices once she found out what sort of life she could be missing. A way to see that things wouldn't be so bad if she just put herself out there.

"So that next time you have a choice to make, you'll have the confidence to make the best one," Abi had said in her most saccharine voice that always made a half-insult sound like a compliment; the not-so-subtle implication that most of Zoe's choices up to this point hadn't been great. To be fair, she wasn't exactly wrong. Zoe was stuck in an office job she hated, with few prospects, no relationship to speak of, and basically no hobbies. At this point, she was ready to try anything.

"That all sounds. . . good," Zoe said.

"Wonderful," Kate beamed. "We just need to cover a few technical things," she handed Zoe the tablet so she could read while she dictated. "For legal reasons, I have to read this out to you." She cleared her throat. "Item one. All questions submitted to ART must be linear and plausible, and should not be based on purely hypothetical scenarios" —Kate paused and went a bit freestyle—"For example, you may not ask *'what if I had dated Ryan Reynolds?'* unless you happen to know him or spent a lot of time in Canada where you might have crossed paths."

She looked at Zoe to confirm, either that she had under-stood, or she had not, in fact, been to Canada in search of Ryan Reynolds or any other famous Ryan for that matter. Zoe shook her head on both counts. "No Ryan Reynolds in my future, got it."

Kate laughed in a stiff sort of way. "Though you never know where the 'what if' you ask will lead," Kate added. "The simulation may surprise you with the familiar or entirely new. A whole alternative world to discover!

Anyway, I digress. Item two: ART limits simulation interactions to four hours per day with a four-session limit per week, to reduce the potential for negative side effects. Which leads me to item three: ART holds no responsibility for any aftereffects experienced, such as confusion, fatigue, migraines, and in some cases, depression, and paranoia. Your file says you have experienced anxiety in the past and data analysis confirms that—is this correct?"

Zoe found her hand jumping to the little medicinal spray she carried in her pocket to help her sleep, and for occasional day-to-day use. She nodded. "Yes, will that be a problem?"

"No, no, that's quite alright. We'll ease you in with short sessions. We understand some people come to AltRealTech as part of a therapeutic journey into their sense of identity and self." She smiled in what looked annoyingly like pity, and Zoe clenched her fists on her lap. She was getting very close to standing up and walking away. She could just tell Abi that it hadn't worked for her, that it wasn't her thing—but it *had* been a kind gesture of her to give her a voucher for the first round of sessions (even if she did get a referral bonus). And Zoe had promised her she'd try harder. She imagined she wasn't the easiest flatmate to live with in her current state of everything-is-shit and what-is-the-point mentality.

"Is everything okay?" Kate asked, her gaze moving between Zoe's clenched hands and the tablet in front of her.

"Yes," Zoe said. "I was just thinking about how excited I am for the experience."

"Great." Kate beamed, staring at Zoe for a few long seconds, then she looked back down at her tablet. "Now, where were we? Yes, our final item, and perhaps an important one for expectation setting. Item Four: While we pride ourselves on greatest market provision, we cannot guarantee full data analysis accuracy, and are unable to offer refunds should alternative experiences not live up to expectations. Do you have any questions?"

"How does it work exactly?"

———————

Kate brought Zoe to an adjacent room with a chair in the centre that gave her instant dentist flashbacks. At least there'd be no pulling teeth here. Kate handed her a heavy white coat with strings around it that looked like it would barely cover her thighs. "When you're ready, lie down on the plinth here. You can set your bag and phone in that box over there. And please turn off all electronics."

"What about my data chip?" Zoe thumbed the small bump under her wrist, the tiny incision scar just a pale freckle. She'd been given it as a toddler along with her usual vaccinations. Most folk got upgrades to ones behind their necks, but Zoe could barely afford a new phone. "I don't have the latest model," she admitted, wondering if it would reduce the treatment experience.

But Kate only shook her head. "Don't worry, we work with every kind of data chip, and we'll deactivate it before we start the process."

"You can do that?" She'd never heard of that being possible outside medical licences.

"Of course! We have been granted exclusive access to data chips for the purposes of the ART experience. Don't worry, it's all above board," Kate said, a little too gleefully.

Zoe raised an eyebrow, but did as she was told, then

reached to take her jumper off. While she stood there in her bra, unbuttoning her jeans, Kate coughed loudly.

"Oh, you can keep your clothes on. The coat is just a precaution."

Zoe blushed, feeling like she was in some alternative universe already—or a rom-com movie, with a manic-pixie-dream girl lead. No meet-cute in this room, unfortunately. "Right, sorry." She fixed herself and hopped up on the plinth.

First, Kate took a small device and scanned it over her wrist where the data chip lived. The device beeped once. "All set," Kate said. "We're going to just do a quick fifteen-minute trial to see how you get on with a basic question. Something like, 'what if I didn't do 'x' yesterday', or 'what if I had watched 'y' movie instead of 'z' at the weekend'. It'll likely be a little dull, but we just want to see how that goes. Can I ask what you did yesterday?"

Zoe took a deep breath. "I sat in my flat for most of the day."

"Right. . . anything else?"

"I went to a coffee shop with my flatmate Abi."

"Wonderful, where was that?"

"Just a small one near us, in the West End."

Kate nodded enthusiastically. "Good, that's good. Now, is there a different café that you often go to, that's not in the West End?"

Zoe thought about it. "There's a place in the Grass-market I used to go more often, but it's not as close to home."

"Wonderful! Okay, when we get you plugged in and sorted, I want you to close your eyes, and think only of your question *'what if I had gone to the Grassmarket café instead of the West End café with Abigail yesterday?'* How does that sound?"

"That sounds wonderful," Zoe said, hoping Kate didn't catch the edge in her voice.

She continued smiling, oblivious. "Excellent, now your flatmate Abigail, that is the Abigail Ellis that we have in our database?"

Zoe made a noise of confirmation, leaning over slightly trying to see Kate's screen, wondering how often Abi had come here, what sort of alternative experiences she'd explored.

"Abigail Ellis," Kate spoke out loud as she typed away on the screen. "And Zoe Young. Okay, Zoe, close your eyes and take some slow deep breaths for me. You might feel a slight pressure around your head, but don't worry, the discomfort will pass once the simulation stops. Ready?"

Zoe closed her eyes and focussed on taking slow deep breaths. Things were being attached to her face. A slight tightening around her head. Her jaw locked.

"Now think about the question," Kate instructed.

Zoe held the question in her mind and began imagining that she'd gone to the Grassmarket café with Abi, over and over. She thought about the mismatched seating, one an old piano with stools pulled up to it, another just an antique trunk. She thought of the cakes in the glass fridges, and the coffees with fancy art on the top. Time passed slowly. How long was she supposed to think about this?

Her thoughts drifted a little. The first time she'd gone to that café was five years ago, when she'd just arrived in Edinburgh. She'd looked in at the bustle and windows brimming with bright cakes and pastries. She had a date with a guy she'd been speaking to on an app—*Adam*. She'd

223

been about to go in, but then Abi had phoned asking if she could come home. She had just broken up with her boyfriend and was crying. Zoe had looked in the window, scanned the faces and spotted a tall guy of around her age, early twenties, rocking a little on his chair in the corner. He was playing with the sleeves of a tartan shirt, a flick of dark hair escaping his otherwise perfectly groomed appearance. She'd been looking forward to going in, but Abi's voice was desperate. "Please Zoe, I-I just need you, *please* come."

"Okay," she'd sighed. "I'll head back now."

With that, she'd taken a final look at Adam and gone home. In hindsight it was a pretty awful thing to do, and when she'd messaged him later to apologise, he hadn't responded. Which she couldn't really blame him for—how long had he waited for her?

What if she'd gone inside and ignored Abi's call?

What if she'd met him that day?

Her mind lurched with a jolt.

Continue reading...

Have You Decided on Your Question is available now in eBook and Paperback direct from Shortwave Publishing or anywhere books are sold.

ACKNOWLEDGMENTS

First, a big thank you to Alan Lastufka. We met through OBSOLESCENCE, which was my first connection with Shortwave – he then took a chance on Have You Decided on Your Question, and again on LIMELIGHT. It's great to find an Editor who both believes in your work, and completely gets what you want to do with it. And it's an extra bonus to work with someone as talented, thoughtful, hard-working, and professional as Alan is. Shout out also to his cover design wizardry!

I'm very grateful to the other Editors who gave many of these stories their first homes – Rob Carroll, Alan Lastufka and Kristina Horner, Alex Woodroe and Cameron Howard, Marissa van Uden, Jonny Pickering, Trevor Quachri, Mark Bilsborough, Craig Kelly, Karen Jones and Damhnait Monaghan, Rebecca E. Treasure, Noel Chidwick and Eris Young, Pete W Sutton, Janice Leagra, Tommy Dean, Monica Mohseni, and Jennifer Lyn Parsons. Thank you for all your editorial guidance, and for believing in my words.

Many of these stories wouldn't be where they are without the invaluable input of various beta readers over the years – Anthea Middleton, Sam Canning, Eris Young, Katalina Watt, Annabel Campbell, Lorraine Wilson, Dave Goodman, Cat Hellisen, C.J. Henderson, Jeremy Pak Nelson, Lindz Mcleod, T.H. Dray and Misha Snowball-Iddon.

A special thank you also to my Mum, who is almost always my first reader, and who never complains when I ask her to listen to my story musings, or to read my dark imaginings (I know she wishes I'd write something happier once in a while, though, sorry Mum!) To my physicist brother, Callum, who sense-checks a lot of my stories, and helps me find solutions to science-related problems – it's very handy as an author to have a brother with Innovations Consultant as a job title! He has also always been extremely supportive of my writing, alongside my Mum and Dad, and much of my extended family. Thank you for always fostering my love of storytelling from a young age.

The book (and probably my writing career) wouldn't exist if I hadn't found my writing community both online and offline. In particular, a thank you to Cymera Fest (and especially Ann Landmann) for fostering such a brilliant SFFH scene in Scotland and beyond, to Edinburgh SFF (you're all amazing), to the teams at Shoreline of Infinity Magazine and Alternative Stories; Fake Realities, to the Scottish Book Trust team, to Skriva, and to all my strangely-named group chats: Scream Team, Funghouls, Mango Appreciation Society, Cosy Club, LFI, and Hooves and Friends – I'm lucky to have such a supportive group of friends and colleagues around me.

Finally, thank you to those who took the time to read and blurb this collection, and to you, reader, for giving these stories a chance – I hope you enjoyed your journey through these near and far dark futures. And for those pushing back against systems that would allow these dark futures to creep closer to reality, thank you and keep fighting the fight – I'll be right there with you.

PREVIOUS PUBLICATIONS

- "Patchwork Girls," *Dark Matter Magazine*, Issue 012
- "Hush, Little Sister," *OBSOLESCENCE*, Shortwave Publishing
- "Rent-A-Baby™: Content Without the Commitment," *Thank You For Joining The Algorithm*, Tenebrous Press
- "Please Select your Issue," *Strange Machines: An Anthology of Dark User Manuals*, Apex Magazine
- "(Un)censored," in *Tangled Web Magazine/Inspiring Fiction*, Issue One
- "We Maintain the Moons," *Analog Science Fiction & Fact*, July/August 2024
- "To Replace a Broken Heart," *Seize the Press Magazine*, Issue #6
- "Space for One," *Wyldblood Magazine*
- "The Gathering," *Shortwave Magazine*
- "Rain Days in Biodome Three," *Scratching the Sands: National Flash Fiction Day Anthology 2023*, National Flash Fiction Day
- "The Bee Bearer," *Shoreline of Infinity*, Issue 34
- "The Medium's Assistant," *BFS Horizons* #16
- "A Ring Around," *Apex Magazine* Issue 143

- "Unfurl," *Janus Literary*
- "The Rift Between Us," *Uncharted Magazine*
- "Crosswords and Coffee," *Calliope Interactive*
- "Sleep Well, My Prince," *Luna Station Quarterly*, Issue 55

ABOUT THE AUTHOR

Lyndsey is a Scottish author of strange and speculative fiction. Her work has appeared in over eighty magazines and anthologies, including with *Apex, Analog, Weird Tales, Flash Fiction Online, Shoreline of Infinity, and PseudoPod*. She's a Scottish Book Trust New Writers Awardee, British Fantasy Award Finalist, and former Hawthornden Fellow. Her novelette *Have You Decided on Your Question* (2023) and collection *Limelight and Other Stories* (2024) are published with Shortwave Publishing. Her novelette *The Girl With Barnacles for Eyes* appeared in Tenebrous Press' *Split Scream* in 2024, and her second collection of Scottish folklore-inspired tales *Dark Crescent* is forthcoming in 2025 from Luna Press. She lives in Edinburgh with her giant kitten Pippin and works in climate change comms in her day job. She's currently working on a number of longer projects in the sci fi, eco fiction, and horror space.

lyndseycroal.co.uk

A NOTE FROM SHORTWAVE PUBLISHING

Thank you for reading! If you enjoyed *Limelight,* please consider writing a review. Reviews help readers find more titles they may enjoy, and that helps us continue to publish titles like this.

For more Shortwave titles, visit us online...

OUR WEBSITE
shortwavepublishing.com

SOCIAL MEDIA
@ShortwaveBooks

EMAIL US
contact@shortwavepublishing.com

CONTENT NOTES

- "Patchwork Girls:" body horror, violence against women
- "Hush, Little Sister:" death of family member
- "Better Self:" disordered eating, fatphobia
- "(Un)censored:" depictions of depression/anxiety
- "Limelight:" abuse, parental control, implication of self-harm
- "To Replace a Broken Heart:" death of a partner, grief
- "Unfurl:" body horror

ALSO AVAILABLE
FROM
SHORTWAVE PUBLISHING

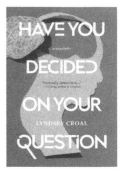

ALSO AVAILABLE
FROM
SHORTWAVE PUBLISHING

ALSO AVAILABLE FROM SHORTWAVE PUBLISHING

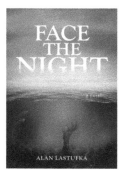

ALSO AVAILABLE FROM SHORTWAVE PUBLISHING

ALSO AVAILABLE FROM SHORTWAVE PUBLISHING

HORROR · SCIENCE FICTION · MYSTERY · DARK FANTASY · THRILLER

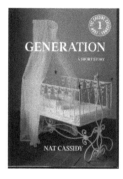

CHAPMAN CHAPBOOKS

CLAY McLEOD CHAPMAN

A series of chapbooks featuring original short stories by Clay McLeod Chapman.

Availabel Titles:

"Mama Bird" is the dark and unsettling tale of a young picky eater and the mother willing to do anything to feed her child.

"Baby Carrots" is the story of a man haunted by a bad batch of produce.

"Knockoffs" are popping up everywhere. Online, on vacation, and—soon—on your block!

FROM THE CASSIDY CATACOMBS

NAT CASSIDY

A series of chapbooks featuring original short stories by Nat Cassidy.

"Generation" - When expecting a new baby, it's normal to have questions. What will my baby look like? What if I'm not ready? What if it's not human? What if this is happening all over? What if this is the end of the world? When expecting a new baby, it's normal to be scared.

Also Available:

"The Art of What You Want"

SHADOWS IN THE STACKS

VINCENT V. CAVA, JAMES SABATA, and JARED SAGE

Shadows in the Stacks is a new horror anthology, published in co-operation with Spirited Giving, to benefit the Library Foundation SD.

Shadows in the Stacks features all-new horror stroies from Clay McLeod Chapman, Jamie Flanagan, Ai Jiang, Jonathan Maberry, Tim McGregor, and more...